APARTMENT 117

First Edition

Published by The Nazca Plains Corporation
Las Vegas, Nevada
2009

ISBN: 978-1-935509-32-5

Published by

The Nazca Plains Corporation ®
4640 Paradise Rd, Suite 141
Las Vegas NV 89109-8000

PUBLISHER'S NOTE
Apartment 117 is a work of fiction created wholly by *Wade Wright's*
imagination. All characters are fictional and any resemblance to any
persons living or deceased is purely by accident. No portion of this book
reflects any real person or events.

Cover Photo, Daniel Korzeniewski
Art Director, Blake Stephens

DEDICATION

This book is dedicated to two former, late, lovers that I do, and will always miss, so very greatly.

Daniel James, my original lover of six and a half years that showed true, absolute unquestionable love and understanding. A man of true value.

And to Earvin LaRuth, my second lover, —of another six and a half years, that truly showed me what a man of the black race, muscular strength, and natural musical talents can truly contribute to the confused world that we all live in.

To both of them, I bow deeply and remind them I will be seeing them in the future.

Wade

APARTMENT 117

First Edition

Wade Wright

CONTENTS

CHAPTER ONE:

The Light in the Bathroom

Sammy answered his front door to see one of the hottest looking maintenance men that he had ever seen! He was tall, built with broad shoulders, a small waist, and showing a very pronounced, and exciting, crotch. Sammy quickly looked the hunk over and made a mental decision that the new maintenance man was one hell of a hot looking man, was probably about 27 or 28 years old, but—damn it, —was wearing a wedding ring.

Sammy was 30 years old, and stood only to about the shoulder height of this adorable hunk of a man, and although he did have a good firm built, it certainly was nothing compared to the muscle man that was now standing directly in front of him at the front door. He knew that he had always admired good looking men in uniform pants, regardless of which type of a uniform, but he quickly decided that this particular pair of pants, with the bulge that was showing, was probably the hottest looking pair that he had ever been up real close to. He quickly noticed that this specific bulge was a little more than just a bulge, —part of what was hidden inside was actually extending down the left leg. This sure made Sammy wonder very quickly if this hunk of a man knew just how much he was showing, did he care, and of course, with that much in his basket area, why didn't he wear briefs so that he could fold it under and kind of hide it?

Sammy had some major concerns about if he had noticed and admired the crotch area a little too long, and had perhaps been seen looking down at it.

"Hi, I'm Jack Jensen, the maintenance man. This is apartment number 117 isn't it? Are you Sam Wilson? I understand you have a light problem somewhere here in your apartment?"

"Yeah, huh yeah." Sammy managed to answer. "The ceiling light in the bathroom went out and even though I put a new bulb in it, it still won't work. Come on in."

Sammy swung the door open as he invited the maintenance man in, and then totally checked his backside out, as Jack entered and went past Sammy. "You are new here aren't you?" Sammy asked.

"Yeah, just started this week. Fact is, I'm still trying to remember which apartments are where. The numbering system for this complex is kind of messed up to me. It doesn't make too much sense."

"Yeah I've always thought that too." Sammy replied, as he eye balled the tall black, mahogany muscular, broad shouldered, statue of a man. He fought to keep his eyes from trailing down to the enormous basket area. He did think to himself, "Damn those pants sure are nice and tight! Damn, I'd love to feel them! Shit, that looks hot!"

"The bathroom is back here," Sammy told Jack.

Jack followed Sammy down the hall toward the bedroom area and into the bathroom.

"So do you live here by yourself?" Jack inquired.

"No, I've got a roommate, but he's not here right now."

"Oh OK." Jack replied. "What's his name?"

"Jim. Jim Nelson." Sammy answered.

"Oh OK." Jack replied as he rather looked around to see what the apartment was like.

"You guys have a nice place here. I've only been in a few of the units so far, but you guys sure have this one fixed up nicer than the other ones I've been in."

"Well thanks!" Sammy acknowledged. "We try! We both like nice stuff."

"Yeah nice stuff like you Mr. Jack Jensen," Sammy said to himself as he watched Jack bed over and put his tool box on the floor. His thought process continued, "Damn one hot maintenance man! What an ass! I hope like hell he stays around for awhile and not the normal two or three weeks, and then off to a better job. Of course with the other ones, who cared, but shit man, this one is way too hot to let go. Oh man! Just freeze yourself there all bent over with your ass and those damn tight pants shining right at my face. Damn man! One hell of a hot ass! Damn, that is good man stuff! Shit, that's hot!!"

Attempting to re-compose himself, and not act like his mind was off, out in the woods someplace, Sammy asked,—as his man of cumin dreams stood back up, "Do you prefer being called Jack, or do you prefer Mr. Jensen?"

"Oh definitely Jack! I always say Mr. Jensen is my Dad! Hey, Sam, do you happen to have a step stool that I could borrow? I did not know this was a ceiling light problem and I did not bring a stool. Have you got one I could borrow?"

"Yeah, sure do Jack. Let me get it for you. It's in the kitchen. I'll be right back."

Sammy headed for the kitchen, retrieved the stool and returned to the bathroom to find that Jack had removed his shirt and was now bare-chested.

"Oh, hope you don't mind," Jack said as he saw Sammy return to the bathroom. "I wouldn't do this if I was in some woman's apartment, but these damn uniform shirts are so damn tight they are hard to move in, so if it's OK with you, since it's just you and me, I'd like to just do without it until I get finished. OK?"

3

"Oh yeah! Yeah—of course it's OK." Sammy replied. Then to himself he continued without actually saying it out loud, "Hell yes you can, and you can take the damned pants off too if you want. Shit man look at those pecs! Look at those biceps! Look at those tinny little nipples! Look at that skin! Shit man, what a hunk! Shit he is hot! Damn he is hot!!! I've never chased after black guys before, but shit man, this one is getting me all turned on!"

Jack opened the stool and after stepping up on it, he proceeded to start work on the lamp fixture. Sammy stood there and with his mouth hanging open, watched Jack reach up and extend his arms above his head. Sammy sighed. Jack heard the sigh and looked toward Sammy.

"You OK?" Jack inquired.

"Oh yeah, I'm OK." Sammy replied. "Yeah, I'm OK."

Turning, Sammy left the hall bathroom and went into the bathroom, off of the main bedroom, and rinsed his face with cold water. He felt that he actually needed to cool himself back down. Jack's naked and exposed upper half, had actually gotten him way too flushed. He grabbed a towel, wiped his face, stood there for a minute or two, and took three deep breaths.

As he returned down the hall to the main part of the apartment, he passed the door to the bathroom where Jack was working. Once again he simply had to stop and gaze at the hunk of this man, that was in his apartment. Actually in his bathroom, half undressed, and while he was in there too! He looked up toward Jack's upper body, and he then looked down toward Jack's waist, and, after loosing self-control, down toward his crotch. Jack saw Sammy looking at this crotch.

Jack smiled, and Sammy immediately turned and left the bathroom area.

Sammy forced himself to stay in the living room and kitchen area, and Jack continued his work on the light fixture.

"There!" Sammy shortly heard Jack exclaim from the bathroom. "It works! Hey Sam, come look. It's working!"

Sammy headed toward the bathroom and as he turned the corner, he saw Jack standing there admiring his handy work, and at the same time rubbing his crotch. Sammy did not know what to look at. The light, or the hand on the crotch. The crotch certainly did hold a greater amount of interest. Right then, Jack's crotch certainly was shinning much more brightly than the light fixture was.

"Hey great!" Sammy said as he came into the bathroom. Jack realized that once again Sammy was eye balling his crotch. And he was giving Sammy a good reason to watch.

"Hey the light man, the light!" Jack said in a rather joking manner. "The light's not your real main interest is it?" Jack asked as he strongly grabbed his crotch, rubbed on it, and then pulled it up after putting his hand down under, and alongside the hang of meat that was going down his left leg.

"What, uhhh, what?" Sammy rather asked.

"Sam, I'm not real ignorant. I think you want to see what I have in my pants, don't you?"

"What!? What!?" Sammy exclaimed! "Why are you saying that?"

"Sam, I know you are a gay guy. I already knew that you had a partner. I already knew his name was Jim. Sam, the only reason I took this job was because I knew this apartment complex has a lot of gay guys in it, and before I go to any apartment, I find out as much about who is there as I can. Why do you think I'd run around without any underwear on? Shit man, I need it to keep everything in there under control. Why do you think I took my shirt off? Hell that shirt ain't that damn tight! I wanted to flex these pecs in front of you and see if I could get you all hot and bothered, and I think I did! I like to mix work and fun together whenever I can, and that's why I like to work in complexes that have a lot of gay guys. I get my rocks off by letting them admire my hours in the gym. Now, want to see what I have hidden down here?" Jack asked, —as he started to unbutton his uniform pants.

"Uhh yeah!" Sammy managed to answer. "Yeah Jack if you want to show me."

Sammy was actually wanting to yell, "Hell yes man! Hell yes I want to see it! Hell yes! Hell yes,—I want to grab it!" But, he was trying to maintain some dignity and not act as if he was as horny as hell, which he was quickly becoming, with the idea in mind, that Jack wanted him to see his dick.

Jack unbuttoned the top button of his uniform pants, and he then told Sammy to finish unbuttoning them and to pull them down. Of course he had no briefs on, which had been very obvious to Sammy ever since he stood at the front door.

"Yeah right man! Yeah, pull 'em down and put 'em down on the floor right on top of my shoes."

Sammy did as he was instructed and found that when he let loose of the pants, he was now face-to-dick with one of the darkest, longest, thickest and one of the sweetest looking dicks that he had ever seen, either in person or in any mag. The skin looked like velvet!

"Oh shit! Oh shit man!" Sammy exclaimed as he backed his face away so that he would be looking at the entire dick and not just the base that was attached to Jack's body. "Damn man! God Jack, you have got the dick of death! Jack, I've never played with a black man's dick before. I've never seen one like this! God Jack,—this thing is enormous!"

"Want to lick it Sam? I've got some time before I'm expected to check back at the office, and I sure do want to make good friends with the people that I will be taking care of around here. Why don't you kind of lick that pole so that I know you and I can be some, good, tight, friends. If I take care of you and your apartment, then I want to know you can take care of me too! See, I've got some tools in my tool box, and I've got this special tool here in my pants! I really want to use this special tool."

Sammy took about three big deep breaths and slowly reached up and took ahold of Jack's bag of balls in his left hand. He took ahold of Jack's cock with his right hand, and then looked up at Jack.

"You aren't even hard yet and this damn thing is almost too damn fat for me to get my hand around. Jack, how damn big does this get when it gets hard?"

"Sam, my young man, you are the one down there with it in your hand. I'm sure if you kind of maybe lick on it and jerk it just a little, it'll start getting hard for you, —so that you can see for yourself! Come on man! Get me hard! I'm feeling kind of horny here, and I need a good looking guy like you to give me some service. I want to watch it disappear right down that hungry mouth of yours. I need to feel your warm, wet, hungry, mouth all over it. Eat my dick man! Use that tool man!"

Sam was shocked that this was happening. He remembered how just a few minutes ago when he first opened the front door to let Jack in, how he was so overtaken by this man's structure and his outstanding form, that at that time he really did want to just throw Jack to the floor and rape him. But now that Jack was telling him to actually do it, Sam was wondering if what was happening was really supposed to be going on. This guy worked for the apartment company, and Sammy was a tenant there. He had never had one of the maintenance men come on to him like this. He was not mentally prepared for this to be happening right then. This was way too unexpected! Hot, but way too unexpected!

Sam looked back down at the black stick of meat and slowly started to move his hand along the shaft. He slightly pulled on the bag of golf balls that were in his left hand. He took a deep breath! He pulled on the bag a little rougher and grabbed his hand around the shaft as far as he could manage. He pushed back on the dick, and felt the skin move along the inner muscle. Then he pulled forward on it and again felt the skin slide. He felt more strength come into the pole. He continued to stroke. He shook his head in amassment as Jack's, black, 'hot rod' got bigger and bigger!

"Oh my God Jack! Jack I never knew a guy could have a dick this damn big! God Jack! Shit man! This damn thing is bigger than any dick I've even seen pictured. Shit Jack, how damn big is this thing?"

"When it's good and hard, like after some good hungry mouth has been on it for awhile, it usually measures about 11 inches long and about six and a half or seven inches around."

"Jack! You said after some hungry mouth has been on it! You mean you have had guys suck on this damn thing? You have had guys that can actually get that in their mouths?"

"Yeah man! Yeah, a lot of guys can! And I don't know why, but it's usually the smaller guys that can take it down their throats and also, those are usually the guys that beg for me to try and ram it up in their asses. The bigger muscle kind of guys usually can't take it in either end. Now Sam, you look like one of the guys that can really take it and enjoy it! Come on man! Let's see if I've started working at the right apartment complex or not. I mean man, if I can't find me enough guys around here to take care of that thing for me, then I will just have to find me another job at another complex where the boys are hungrier and more anxious to make Mr. Jack and his big, black, long, dick, happy! I know from past experience, I need serviced, by a guy, at least once a day, so I've got to get my men lined up. Sam, I want you to be one of them!"

Sam let loose of the bag of balls and placed both hands on Jack's dick. He started stroking it with both hands clasped together as far as possible. His face was directly in front of the dick and he was stroking back and forth, aiming directly at his own face.

"Yeah that's the way man!" Jack said. "Yeah that's starting to feel reaaaaaal good Sam. Grab it tight and stroke it hard! Let me know you have ahold of it! Let me feel it! I want to get it as big for you as I can, so you need to start getting a little more rough on it. Stroke me man! There is a lot of meat down there to get all excited. Come on man, beat me off some. Get it all excited! Get me good and hard!"

Sammy caressed Jack's dick and rubbed his face up against the side of it as he stroked it back and forth. Slowly but firmly it stretched out and started to reach its maximum size. To Sammy it actually felt like a steel baseball bat in his hand. He moved his mouth to the tip of it. He opened his mouth as wide as possible. He slowly and with hesitation moved his mouth onto the end of Jack's over-sized rod. Sammy knew it would be a total challenge to get part of, if not most of, Jack's meat into his mouth.

Grabbing ahold of Jack's hips, Sammy forced his face forward and pulled on Jack's body in an attempt to swallow as much of the big meat sausage as possible.

Jack placed his hands on the back of Sammy's head and slowly and deliberately pulled his head toward himself. Sammy gulped and gagged as he allowed Jack to force his head onto the big meat stick. He had to pull his head back to allow himself to get some air, and while he was off of the dick, he said, "Oh shit man! Oh shit this damn thing is way too big!"

As soon as he had made his statement of qualifying the dick as too big, Sammy immediately threw his face forward and once again forced as much of the black cock back into his mouth and as far down his throat as possible. Sammy had now had enough of his, —attempting to take it, —and he had now turned very anxious to get all of it, if at all possible. He had been hesitant when he started, but he was now hot and ready to force himself to take it even if it was uncomfortable to do it. He realized that for some unknown reason, he trusted Jack enough, that even though he knew he would not be able to breathe, Jack wouldn't let him suffocate. He forced his mouth open, and he forced the dick inside as far as possible. The dick head was way more than anything he had ever attempted to put in his mouth. He rammed his face forward. Jack pulled Sammy's head onto his dick. Sammy's throat was completely filled. It was being spread open.

Sammy sucked and licked the enormous piece of meat. Jack used Sammy's head as a jerk-off device. With his hands firmly placed on each side of Sammy's head, he forced Sammy's mouth on and off of his dick until he finally said, "Hey—man! I'm getting real ready! Sam, I'm getting real, real close! Man, I'm about to shoot! I'm getting real close to cumin! Hey guy, I'm going to shoot! Sam, Sam, you want it in your mouth?"

Suddenly Jack's whole body went rigid! He thrust his crotch toward Sammy. He pulled on Sammy's head! Every muscle tightened up! He stood there without saying anything and his entire being went as rigid as a marble statue.

9

Sammy knew that when Jack's dick shot, it was going to be a very big load. He decided that a dick that big couldn't do anything but shoot big loads, and with his actions on that dick, he had gotten himself so excited, about getting the chance to play with a dick that big, that he was now getting really anxious and excited about taking the full load down his throat. He tried to utter, "OK, OK," but with his mouth so full and spread so far open, he had trouble getting the words out. He was not about to take the dick out of his mouth to say anything. He did not want to find his face or chest getting the shot gun load that he was now wanting to feel hit the back of his mouth.

Jack shot! Jack shot big! Jack shot strong! Sammy pushed his face onto Jack's dick as far as he could go. Sammy moaned and groaned as he tried to swallow the man-milk as fast as he could. Jack stood there completely rigid and continued to shoot. Shot after shot! Sammy continued to swallow.

Finally Jack's dick quit shooting, and he slowly allowed his body to relax. Sammy swallowed the remaining cum that he still had in his mouth. He pulled his mouth back from the forced position that he had assumed, the position that he had used so that he made sure he got all of this handsome man's juices. He felt like he had drank the city water well dry. He had never had a dick that big in his mouth before, he had never taken that much cum before, and he had never had a black man fuck his face before. He thought, "Now I know why they say, —Go Black, you never go Back!"

Sammy pulled off of Jack's dick. He wiped his mouth with the back of his right hand. He looked up at Jack and exhaustingly said, "Shit, oh man! Oh shit! God Jack, you loaded me fucking full! God Jack! You must have shot a quart of juice into my mouth! Man, I had trouble swallowing it fast enough! God man, you have got one hell of a hot dick!"

"Well, —Sammy my man!" Jack replied, after regaining some composure and strength. "I certainly have found myself a guy that knows how to take it, use it, and eat it! You had fun on my cock, didn't you guy?"

Sitting back on his heels, grabbing the sides of Jack's tree trunk legs, he looked up at Jack and tried to say, "Oh hell yes I did Jack. Jack I've never had that much cock in my mouth all at once before. Oh shit man! Oh, when you started cumin I had to swallow as fast as I could! Oh shit man! Oh man, you loaded me full! Yeah, Jack, yeah I do have to admit that I had fun. I'm fucking exhausted, but shit yes, I had fun! Jack, I need to catch my breath!"

"So I guess maybe that might mean that when I need to get my nuts off, I can stop by here and let you take care of it for me? Right? Can I count on you as one of my main men on sucking me off when I need it?"

"Well Jack, I guess so, but I do have a partner, remember? We don't usually fuck around without the other guy being here, so I'm not so sure about just any ole time. I really didn't expect anything like this to happen today. I've never had some maintenance man kind of strip himself down, show me all of his muscles, and then pull his enormous big thick dick out and offer it to me before. God Jack, especially one like that! Jack, the way you look and the way you are built, I'm sure you can do that to just about any guy and he'll go for it, but I did not intend to make hay with somebody without Jim being here. I'm not so sure I should be doing this again. I'm not so sure that would be fair to Jim. God Jack! I'm getting real confused here! Jack you are so hot! So fucking hot! God having sex with you is way too much to believe. Jack, you said you need a guy to do you at least once a day? My God Jack! I can see why you need multiple guys! I don't think one guy could do this everyday! Jack, I want to, but —Oh, I don't know!"

"So how about we set it up so that I can meet your Jim, and see if maybe we can do a three-way or something. Hey, Jim might be more agreeable to letting you suck me off when I need it if he and I know each other. Is Jim a good sucker? Does he go for sucking on big dicks? Maybe he'd like to suck me off too! Maybe I can line both of you guys up for me! Will he suck on a big black dick? Will he do black dick?"

"Oh Jack. This is getting so confusing! Yeah, I'd really like a three way with you and Jim, and yeah, I know I'd like to have more sex with you later, but man! But, —Jack, —I don't know if all you like is just getting sucked off or if you like other stuff too. I mean, to have a three way and have one of the guys just wanting to get himself sucked off, —well that doesn't usually work too well. What else are you into? Anything else, or just getting sucked off? Hey, please tell me you like more stuff, cause I sure do know that Jim sure does not have any problems playing around with big dicks, and I know he likes black, and I know that if he can get to a big long black one like yours, he's gonna be game, big time game!"

CHAPTER TWO:

That Nice, Tight, White, Firm Ass

"Jim, there's the door bell, —Jim answer the door. Jack's here!"

"This guy had better be as damn hot as you said! I trust you, —but man, —this guy had better look like a mahogany God!" Jim rather quietly 'yelled' back toward Sammy as he left the living room and headed for the door.

As Jim answered the door, Sammy came running up behind him, and as the door came open, Sammy said, "Hi Jack! Jack, meet Jim, and Jim, —meet Jack."

Jim dropped his jaw, he took a deep breath, and he attempted to extend his right hand out to offer a hand shake. Slowly, and breathlessly he managed a, "Hi! Hi, I'm Jim."

Jack was dressed for making a major impression! No uniform pants nor shirt this time! A skin tight, tit hugging, chest kissing painted on dark red tank top, and a pair of cuffed up shorts that looked like they should be on some young junior high aged kid that hadn't started growing up yet! Jim took one look at him and immediately thought, "Oh shit man! How in the hell can he walk up steps in those tight assed, dick hugging shorts let alone sit down! Oh shit man, I wish I had been the guy to pull 'em on for him!"

"Jim he knows you are Jim. I just introduced you to him. Jack, come on in. Jim, close your mouth and take Jack into the living room while I get some snacks from the kitchen. OK? Hey—Jim—are you in there?"

Jim's statement that this guy had better be a 'mahogany God,' had just been answered. He managed to step out of the way and let Jack enter the apartment, and then went with Jack into the living room. Sammy looked at his partner, laughed and shook his head. Then asked, "So, my man! Did I describe him correctly or not?"

Jim escorted Jack into the living room, waited for Jack to be seated, stood there still with his mouth hanging rather open and said, "Well, I've accused Sammy of lying to me for the last time! I sure as the hell can see that! Jack, I'm sorry that I am acting like such a fool, but I simply kept telling Sammy that his description of you had to be a little too much made up. When I agreed to his constant begging that I meet you and see if maybe we could do a three-way together, I was just real sure he was kind of making you out to be something a little more than you really were."

Then turning toward the kitchen, Jim grinningly yelled, "Sammy, I'm sorry. I'm real sorry honey. From this time on I will always believe everything that you tell me." Turning back to Jack he continued, "See Jack, —once in awhile he kind of gets all excited about how hot some guy is, and then when I finally see that guy, he's not as hot as I had been told. So I'm sorry but I thought this was another one of those times. Shit man, I was wrong! Holly crap was I wrong! Jack, you are one hot looking guy! Now I understand why Sammy was all turned inside out, upside down, with excitement that day you came over here to fix that light fixture. Man, when I got home that night he was a complete basket case! I sure as hell understand now why he was as flustered as he was. Shit man! If I'd been him, I'd probably been more flustered than he was!"

Sammy carried some cheese, crackers and beers into the room, sat them down on the coffee table, looked at Jim, snickered, and said, "OK! I will accept the payment of your, —'million dollar statement', any time you wish to write the check."

Jim looked at Jack and explained. "During his excited description of what you were like, I was kind of loosing my patience and told him that I bet a million dollars that you are not even half of what he was telling me. Got to admit man, that is one bet I would have lost!"

"Well guys!" Jack responded. "Guys, I'm glad I'm OK with you guys, but hey, I'm just me. Sure, I do try to show myself off when I can, but hey man, like they say, I still put my pants on one leg at a time like everybody else."

As Jim reached over to get some cheese and crackers, he added, "Well, from what Sammy has told me, those pants can come off pretty damn quickly too!"

Jack snickered, reached over for a beer and some cheese and crackers and then after sitting back in his chair, looked at Jim and said. "Well Jim, I certainly did not have any reason to doubt Sammy's description about you, and from what I now see, he really was on target describing you. You've obviously spent some time in the weight room too haven't you?"

"Yeah." Jim replied. "Yeah I have. Sure did not do for me what it did for you, but I do have to admit that I am sure I do look better than if I hadn't done the old weight room thing. When I was younger I needed to put weight on, but then after I got just a little older, the goals started working the other direction."

"Sammy said you are what—34? Is that right?"

"Yeah, I've got a birthday coming up shortly, but right now I'm still 34. You are what—28, 29? I'm not sure Sammy knew, for sure."

"I'm 29, a horny 29."

"Well the horny part we already knew about! But after what Sammy told me about the actions in our bathroom the other day, it kind of sounded like if you had not been on the horny side, you might have been raped anyway!"

"Jim!" Sammy snapped back rather humorously. "Jim, you make it sound like I was all over him!"

"Well, you did kind of keep looking at my crotch while I was trying to keep my mind on fixing that light!" Jack did add.

"Jack, dear Sir!" Sammy replied. "Sir,—I would have been a lot more calm about you being in my bathroom if you had not been half naked, had not flexed those 20 inch biceps in my face, had not shown me those tight thick pecs, and had kept your hand off of that damn telephone pole you were rubbing! Shit man—all of you that day was way too much for me to handle! I was afraid that you were gonna have to call 911 for me, after I passed out from just looking at you, and watching you rub that dick of yours!"

"So Jack," Jim asked, "Sammy told me that he knew for sure, you sure do like to have your big, stiff, thick, rod sucked off good, but when he asked you what else you liked to do, you just told him something like, —well,— time will tell, but you guaranteed him that he would not be disappointed. What did you mean by that?"

"Yeah, I know he was concerned about us doing a three-way and maybe me being only interested if I get sucked off. I'm not sure just what all you guys are into, but I'm sure I've done enough stuff that most of it's not going to be anything new to me. But, the longer we sit here and just talk about it, the longer it will be, in finding out just what I do like to do. Are we going to go play, or just sit here and talk?"

With that remark and question, all three men immediately got up, and headed down the hall toward the bedroom. As they got into the bedroom, all three pulled their shirts off and Jack looked at Jim and remarked, "Shit man! Hey, you really are stacked aren't you? Sam told me you had a hot body, but shit man, he didn't tell me you were that hot. You have spent a lot of time in the gym haven't you?"

"Yeah, I've spent my time there. Thanks for the complement, but I do have to admit I wish I looked like you do. Shit man, —look at that fucking ass on you! Shit man, how in the hell does any man get an ass that fucking hot looking? Shit man, God that is nice!"

Jack, Jim and Sammy all got fully undressed and after just a little confusion of just who was going to lay down where and beside who, they managed to stretch out together with Jack in the middle. Jim reached over and massaged Jack's right pec. As he massaged it, he then raised up and placed his lips on the nipple and slowly and gently started chewing and sucking on it. He rolled his tongue around in circles on it. Jack kept lowly saying, "Thank you man, thank you man!"

Jack reached down and grabbed ahold of Jim's stiff and thick 8" man tool. He jerked on it, pulled on it, and made Jim moan and groan in delightful pleasure as he sucked on Jack's nip.

As soon as they had gotten in position in bed, Sammy quickly positioned his mouth on Jack's large, massive, thick, steel hard dick! It was already large, larger than most men's after theirs is completely hard, but he knew this one would get bigger yet. He had experienced it before, and he was eager for it again. This time, he managed to slam the entire length down into his throat much faster than he had done just a few days earlier. This time his mouth and the back of his throat were ready for it. He now knew how relaxed he needed to be to take the entire thing. As he pushed his face down onto Jack's crotch, and swallowed the entire length of this thick, black, dick, he took a deep breath of air through his nose, and then after coming back up and off of it, told Jim, "Man, you have got to do this! This damn thing is so good! Oh Jim, you've got to eat this one. This is like swallowing a whole chocolate factory all at once!"

With an extensive amount of feeling, licking, groping, hugging, chewing, and sucking, the three men completely enjoyed each other's bodies for more than an extended period of time. Each had been acting as if they were three little kids playing in a sandbox!

After Sammy had choked himself completely a couple of times on Jack's big turned on and excited, stiff, beef stick, he offered it to Jim, and told Jim he really did want to see just how much of it Jim could swallow on his first try. Jim finally did take all of Jack's dick down his throat, but only with a lot of care and patience! Sammy had told him that to take it all, "You've got to force that damn thing down your throat if you really want to take all of it. Jim, it's not going to go down your throat easily. It will make you gag! You've got to push your face on it! You will swear you have never had that much in your mouth all at once before, and I'm sure you haven't!"

Jack laid back and offered his stick to the two lovers that he was now enjoying some fantastic bedroom time with. As Jim learned how to get his mouth completely down onto this enormous, enormous, dick, Jack massaged the top of his head, and at the same time massaged all and any parts of Sammy's body that he could reach. Jack was being taken care of by his new lover friends, and he was enjoying each and every moment of it! He knew his body was being worshipped. He knew his body, his enormous dick, and all of his muscles had been worshipped many times before, but this act of being loved, and body handled by two men in love with each other, was especially exciting to Jack. He knew that neither one of them needed him for some good sex. They, each, already had a very hot looking man at their respective disposal.

As Sammy watched his lover learn how to take all of Jack's dick, he offered encouragement and support and eventually turned himself around in the bed so that he was now laying with his feet up by Jack's head, and his bare butt sticking up in the air. As he encouraged Jim to, "Swallow deeper, swallow deeper," he felt Jack's hand start to slide in between the cheeks of his ass. He laid his head down and moaned, "Oh yeah! Oh yeah, please! Oh yeah Jack please finger fuck me!"

Jack followed instructions. His left hand was now exploring Sammy's firm and solid ass muscles. He grabbed it and squeezed it. Slowly one finger found the tight entrance into Sammy's insides. "Yeah push! Yeah push!" Sammy pleaded and begged for more and more ass action. He was in glory!

Jack pulled his hand back toward himself, spit on his fingers and once again went back to the tight little hole that Sammy was offering so eagerly. Jack reached down, entered one finger, ran it around in circles and then told Sammy, "Hey relax man. Relax your ass. I want to put some more fingers up in there!"

Sammy tried to relax his ass and as he did, Jack let him have one more finger. "Yeah, relax man! Yeah, relax," he told his buddy. He was now fingering with two rather large fingers. "Yeah I like that!"

Slowly he inserted finger three, then finger four! Sammy wiggled and moved his ass slowly letting Jack know that he could feel all of the fingers and that although his rather full ass was kind of hurting, he was still wanting more of the actions that he was being given.

Suddenly Sammy realized that he could not see Jim's left hand anyplace, and after some rather stressing stretching and looking, he finally realized that while he was getting Jack's fingers stuck up into his ass, Jim was doing the same thing to Jack's ass!

"Holy crap!" Sammy exclaimed. "Shit man! I didn't know you had your hand up in his ass! Shit man! Damn I did not know that!"

Jim could not answer more than a groan of something like a "Yeah," since he had a mouth full of cock. Jack did respond. "Yeah man he does and it feels damn good! He was sticking fingers in my ass hole before I started on yours. Yeah—and it feels damn good!"

As Jack laid there and got his ass fingered, he fingered Sammy's ass, and Sammy reached over and got Jim to move over toward him, so that he could suck on Jim's dick. Jim sucked on Jack's dick. All of it! All three men were in complete joy of having some good hot gay sex play with a couple of other really hot, and ready guys.

"I want to fuck a hole!" Jack suddenly said. "I want some ass!"

That statement rather broke up all of the actives that were then happening. Jim looked at Sammy, Sammy looked at Jim, and Sammy finally was the one that said, "Oh shit man! Oh God, he wants to stick that damn big thing up in one of us!"

Jim immediately replied, "Well let me tell you man, you are the one that found this guy, and so I figure it's up to you to see if a guy's ass can take that much dick. You lay your ass down here and I

19

will be your cheering section. I'll watch you take it, and then if you can take it without getting ripped open from one end to the other, them maybe,—and I said—maybe—I will try it!"

Everything got stopped and everybody repositioned themselves for the upcoming fucking. Sammy asked Jack in what position he wanted him, and Jack told him to lay on his stomach and just relax. Jim sat down up by Sammy's head and spread his legs, one on each side of Sammy's face so that he could place his crotch right at Sammy's face, with the intent that as Sammy got it in the rear, he could suck Jim off at the same time.

Jack used some of the KY lube that Jim and Sammy had on the night stand, and he slowly positioned himself above Sammy's ass. He laid down on Sammy's back and let his enormous dick slide in between the cheeks of Sammy's ass. He moved himself up and down a few times so that Sammy could feel the entire length of his dick rubbing along Sammy's skin. He anticipated, and correctly so, that doing that would get Sammy all anxious and excited for getting it up in his ass. As he moved, he watched Sammy reach out and get ahold of his partner's dick and put it in his mouth. That action was a good signal to Jack that Sammy was getting all sexy excited and was not particularly afraid of what was about to happen back in his ass.

Jack reached in-between Sammy's ass cheeks and inserted a finger. After rubbing it around some, he then inserted finger number two, then three and then finger four. He spread his fingers apart as far as possible to start spreading open Sammy's rectum. As he played with his fingers, he watched Sammy's actions on Jim's dick, and also watched Jim's expressions to give himself a good indication of how Sammy was reacting to the fingering and the spreading that was happening in his butt. He knew that if anything was hurting, his reaction on Jim's cock would change, and Jim's expression would follow suit. Nothing was going wrong! All actions were on track. Jack was spreading Sammy's ass hole as far as his fingers could manage, and Sammy was completely involved in sucking on Jim's stiff dick.

Jack withdrew his fingers and as he did, he looked up at Jim. Jim grinned. He knew what was about to happen and he was letting

Jack know that he was "instep" with what was happening. Sammy was anxiously sucking on the dick that he had so completely rammed into the back of his throat.

Jack raised his torso up high enough to get his dick out from in-between Sammy's ass muscles, and he took ahold of it enough to aim it toward Sammy's, now anxious and hungry ass. He placed the tip at the rose point opening, that had already started to close itself back up. Jack allowed the tip of his cock, to touch its target. He pushed! He slid his hands around Sammy's chest. He squeezed. He allowed more of his dick to push into the small opening ever so slightly. He laid his head down on the bed beside Sammy's face. He laid there for a moment listening to Sammy suck on Jim's dick. He could not only hear the sucking but he could also feel the actions since his head was immediately beside it. He enjoyed his position, and his closeness, to one man sucking off his loving partner. He felt privileged to be so close to such personal and loving actions.

Jack lowered his torso down. He allowed his dick to punch in. Sammy jerked and groaned. Jack looked up at Jim, and quickly got an understanding that everything was OK. Jim shook his head in a "Yes" motion so to tell Jack that everything was still OK, and to keep pushing. Jack did. He thrust his torso so that another three or four inches of his railroad tank-car sized dick would go on into Sammy's, "shit shoot". Just as quickly as he mentally phrased that term, the "shit shoot," he regretted that he ever thought of Sammy's ass in that type of a term. He had thought of other guy's asses in that term, but he did not like thinking of Sammy's ass that way.

He was unhappy that he could even think of that nice, tight, white, firm ass, in such a negative way. He was actually making love to it. It was making him feel very good and very, very, manly, so how could he be so negative as to even think of it in such a negative term. He immediately decided that instead of looking at it as a "shit shoot," he much preferred referring to it as a nice, warm, moist, cock glove. He did know that Sammy did use it as his "shit shoot", but right now it was being shared with him as a very exciting cock glove. And a very firm fitting cock glove. One cock glove that felt like a leather glove, turned inside out, and Sammy was letting him slide his excited, stiff dick into the tight leather compartment of that glove.

Jim took ahold of Sammy's head and pulled him forward, as much as possible. Actually, since Sammy was completely up and on Jim's lower stomach, Jim's pulling on his head did not actually move him any, but it definitely did lock him in place. Jim knew that Jack was just about ready to give Sammy's ass the rest of that oversized mahogany meat and he knew Sammy would be reacting whenever that thing hit its full extent. He knew Sammy would try to pull off of his dick and let out some kind of a scream. He looked at Jack, and motioned an "OK". Jack rammed! He slammed his body down onto Sammy's ass. He squeezed Sammy's chest as he pushed. He groaned as if he was the person getting it up in the ass.

Sammy jerked! He attempted to pull off of Jim's dick, but Jim held him tight! He tried to yell, —he could not, —he had a mouth full of Jim, and Jim was pulling on him tightly! He turned and twisted his body. He attempted to flip and twist and turn! He continued to attempt some yelling, but nothing happened. Jack pushed in farther! Jack pushed strongly, so as to make sure he was staying completely embedded into the depths of Sammy's ass hole. Embedded to its fullest! He completely and very strongly controlled all of Sammy's attempted movement. He made Sammy his capture! He simply knew that if he and Jim could manage to control Sammy for only about 10 or 15 seconds, the sharp pain would diminish and Sammy would then be begging for more dick up his ass. Jack had enough prior experiences, with other tight sweet ass holes, to simply know that if he can keep his bottom boy under a complete control, and not allow that ass to escape, or to even make an attempt to come off of his rod, that within only a few seconds that ass will not only quit hurting, but it will immediately feel as if it is only partly filled. It will be much more anxious now, for more dick, a lot more dick, than the man getting fucked had even been hoping for, just before he started getting any sharp painful feelings.

Jim had complete control of Sammy's head, and Jack had complete control of the rest of Sammy's body. They looked at each other, and as they did, Sammy became very calm. He allowed his entire body to totally relax, and he then rested all of himself, on the bed.

Jim released his grip on Sammy's head. Jack pushed his dick in again, just to make sure he was in the full way. He loosened his grip around Sammy's body. He asked, "You OK? You OK?"

Sammy took his mouth off of Jim's dick and managed a low volume, "Yeah! Oh shit man! Oh shit, that hurt for a moment. God Jack! Is that just your dick, or did you put something else up in there too? Is that just your dick or is part of your hand up in there?"

"Hey man, that is just my dick! You told me the other day when I was here that you liked the looks of it and wondered what it would feel like up in your ass, well tell me, what does it feel like? It's up in your ass now!"

"Oh shit, OK I guess. I need to rest a little and then I will let you know. Shit man, when you pushed the rest of it up in me, how much did you push in me then. Was that the whole thing. I thought you already had some of it in me, but shit man, that felt like you must have rammed the entire thing up in there."

"No! I already had about half of it up in you. You just took the second half of it when I pushed."

Sammy then looked at Jim's dick and asked, "Are there any teeth marks on your dick Honey? I know damn well that when he punched the rest of that rod up in me, I bit your dick hard. I remember having that pain hit inside of my ass, and how it just went right up through my body and that's when I clamped my mouth shut on your dick and tried to yell. Is your dick OK? Did I bite your dick any?"

"Yeah Honey, my dick is OK! I knew you were about ready to get it back there, so when it hit and then you bit, I wasn't surprised. I expected it. Jack had looked at me with kind of a look of, OK, Here goes! So I knew things were going to happen. Are you OK? Is your ass OK, or does it still hurt?"

"Hell no it doesn't hurt now! It's fine. Everybody has always said that if you get it up in the ass by some dick that is really kind of too big, that once you have it up in you for a little while, that then you don't even feel full anymore, and you start begging for more. I kind of guess that must be true, because right now that dick of Jack's feels so damn good up in there, and I'm hoping that he's got more to give me. My ass feels real good and hungrier now than it was before." Then, turning to try and look at Jack, he continued, "Jack, you do have more to put up in me don't you? Jack, please tell me you are only about halfway up in me!"

"Sorry, — hungry little ass boy! You have all of me up in you right now, but what will help you out some is for me to do some hot hard fucking. Ever since I got it up in you, I've just laid here nice and still so that you and your cute little white ass could get used to it. Now that you know your ass hole is OK and it's not going to get all ripped open, now it's time for me to get myself all cock excited and get myself ready to load your ass with some home grown lube. You about ready to see how much ass fucking you can take? I want to fuck you harder than any ass I've ever fucked before!"

Jim grinned and said, "Yeah Jack, he's ready! You are ready aren't you Sammy? Do it Jack! He's been anxious for that dick of yours ever since he saw it the other day, and I know he is really begging for it mentally right now!"

"Yeah fuck me! Yeah—fuck me please Jack! Oh Jim, hold me please. Jim, don't let him get too rough on my ass, please!" Sammy pleaded.

Without further comments, Jack immediately started using his rod the way he liked to use it the most. He started in on Sammy's ass and used it to the fullest. He was hoping for a rougher fuck on Sammy than any other guy had ever allowed him to do. He felt comfortable with going for the roughest ever since he also had Jim there and taking care of Sammy, and Sammy's ass. He kept watching Jim for any input that he needed to be aware of. He knew that if he was getting too rough on Sammy, that Jim would know and would give him the hint to kind of ease up. As he fucked, cock punched and cock slammed Sammy's ass, he got no indications that he needed to change his actions. The exciting input, was hearing Sammy utter, "Yeah, man! Yeah!" He knew from hearing that, Sammy was OK, and was really enjoying getting his ass fucked probably harder, faster and deeper, than he had ever had before. He knew he had found himself a good active ass to play with. One that was deep enough, and hungry enough, to be anxious for this action again, as soon as possible and as often as possible.

As Jack was sweating profusely from his forehead, he suddenly started yelling out that he was getting close. "I'm getting close guys! I'm getting close! Hey—man! I'm getting real ready! Sammy, I'm getting real, real close! Men, I'm about to shoot! I'm getting real close to cumin! Hey guys, I'm going to shoot! I'm cumin! I'm cumin! I'm cummmmmin!"

Suddenly Jack's whole body went rigid! He thrust his crotch forward into Sammy, forcing his rod to go into Sammy as deeply as possible. He pulled on Sammy's body! Every muscle tightened up! He laid there on, and in, Sammy's ass without saying anything and his entire being, once again, went as rigid as a marble statue. Sammy could feel his ass being filled with Jack's warm cream fluids. He realized how similar this was to the day that Jack shot off down his throat; how Jack had made the exclaimed statement about getting really close, and then how completely his body went totally rigid as his natural actions and reactions, took over and his body released the sexual fluids that he had been building up as he either pumped Sammy's face, or today, as he force fed his ass with every bit of force that he could offer with his beautiful, beautiful big black dick.

Sammy collapsed onto Jim's lap, and Jack completely collapsed on Sammy's back. Everybody took deep breathes attempting to rather re-group after the most fierce fuck session that any of the three men had ever been involved in.

Sam finally uttered, "Oh shit Jim, I think I just got fucked! Oh shit Jim, I think my insides are all messed up. Oh shit man, I've never been fucked like that before. Jim, I always thought you got pretty rough on me, but shit man, we just found ourselves a real rough fucker. Jim, you've got to get fucked by him, oh shit man! What a great feeling!"

"Sammy, my dick is starting to get soft. I'm going to pull it out." Jack said.

"Oh Jack, push it back up in me as much as you can before you pullout, —please! I want to feel it up in there as far as you can go again, please!"

Jack pushed his body toward Sammy's ass as far as he could, and then pulled back and let his dick escape from what he had earlier referred to as the cock glove. As it came out, Jack leaned down and gave Sammy's shoulder blades a kiss, and then reached up and gave Jim a good long and meaningful full lip kiss.

"Men!" He said so very quietly. "Men, I have never had sex like this before. I love being in bed with both of you two. Men, this is way too exciting to even try and explain how I feel. Sammy, —your ass OK?"

"Oh yeah, my ass is OK, —just feels kind of empty right now, though! Yeah Jack, I know I sure enjoyed this! Jim didn't get it in the ass like I did, but the next time, you fuck him OK? I want to watch you fuck him! I want to be in a position where I can watch that dick go up in his ass."

The men all got up, they each took quick showers, (to their regret, the apartment shower was not large enough for all three men at the same time), and as they were re-dressing, Jack then said, "Well men. I sure do hope I've got some sex left in me after that session. My little wifey will be home from work shortly, and if I don't act horny when she gets there, then I will be in for about an hour of questions about how I spent my day and evening. Can't do that! So, I guess I will just have to look at this session as a warm up for some good ole straight sex at home. Hey, next Friday about the same time? Right? Is that what we agreed? Hell, my head was still going in circles from that much fucking when we talked about it, so I had better be sure I know what we decided."

"Yeah next Friday and about 7:00." Jim replied.

"OK. And Mr. Jim, — from what your partner has indicated, it will be my dick up in your ass, that time! OK?"

"Well, —we'll see!" Jim answered. "I know what Sammy went through getting that damn telephone pole of yours up in his ass, and he is a hell of a lot more used to getting fucked than I am, so I will have to think about that!"

"OK, you decide. If you want it, I'll go easy on you, but if you decide against it, then maybe you two will double fuck me, instead! OK?"

CHAPTER THREE:

My Little Act Worked, Didn't It?

Jack approached the door to apartment 234, hit the door bell and waited for somebody to answer the door. Mark did.

"Hi, I'm Jack Jensen, the maintenance man. Are you Mark Jenkins?" Jack asked as he looked at his work-order.

As Mark stood there with his mouth not exactly clamed shut, he replied that "Yes, I'm Mark Jenkins."

"I've got a work-order here that you have some kind of a shower problem. Is this a convenient time for me to come in and check it out?" Jack asked.

"Well not actually," Mark replied. "I've got to take my wife to work. She's got to be there by one, and then I can come back. Can you come back in, oh, —maybe 15 or 20 minutes, and give me time to take her to work. Then it would be OK, —is that OK? See, I've got to take her to work, and then I'll be back here. Is that OK?"

Jack realized that Mark did seem to be having some small problems of trying to get his mind all organized and in order, trying to explain that a little later would be better. Jack noticed that Mark was rather interested, or had lost control, in letting his eyes run rapidly up and back down the front of him, as he tried to get the words out, in somewhat of an organized manner.

"Yeah, that will be OK." Jack said. "I've got some stuff that needs to be done that will only take me a few minutes anyway, so I'll go do that and then come back in about half an hour. OK?"

Jack left the door and immediately headed for apartment 117. He rang the door bell. Sammy answered the door.

"Sammy. You busy? You home by yourself?"

Sammy answered. "No Jack, I'm not busy. Yeah, I'm home alone. What's up man?" Sammy opened the door and allowed Jack to come in.

"Sammy, can I take a real quick shower here? I feel like I am really dirty and stinky, and I'd like to kind of freshen up if it's OK with you."

"Well yeah of course you can Jack, but what in the hell is the deal? You don't look dirty or smell funny. What's happening?"

"Sammy, what do you know about that Mark Jenkins guy up in apartment number 234? Do you know him?"

"No Jack, I have no idea of who he is. Why? What's going on here, man?"

"Sammy I got a job order for his apartment for a shower problem, and I just went over there to see if I could come in to fix it. Mark came to the door, and I'm telling you Sammy, he had trouble talking to me. His eyes went up and down on me the whole time I was standing there. He told me—well kind of—that he had to take his wife to work, and he asked me to come back in 15 or 20 minutes after he gets back. Sammy, I have been around enough guys to know that if his wife is not going to be home, the way he ate me up with those eyes, —when I get in there, —I've got a good chance of maybe getting me some good virgin male ass! Sammy, I'm serious. I just know the way he was acting at that door, I've got me a good chance, for some fresh ass meat when I go back there! I want to make sure I'm all good and clean and not gross smelling, so can I use your shower?"

"Hell yes Jack. Shit yes! Tell me about this guy. Is he hot looking? Well—I kind of guess he must be, as excited as you are about maybe getting to him."

"Yeah Sammy. He is hot looking! Looks like he is in his mid twenties. He has a body! He had on a tight white sleeveless T-shirt, and a pair of Levis. I didn't get a chance to see the butt of those jeans, but from the looks of the front, I'm sure the back is going to be one hell of a hot picture. Sammy, I've got to see if I can roll with this guy. I've hardly ever gone for getting to some married guy, I usually just go after the gay guys since I know they always want it, but Sammy, this guy is hot and I swear he is ready! Hey,—maybe he has played around before, I don't know, but I sure am going to see if I can lay him if at all possible!"

Sammy gave Jack a towel to use, and of course made himself available to do the drying so that he was absolutely sure that Jack had gotten himself all good and dry, which was his 'reasoning' for insisting that he do the drying for Jack. Of course,—accidentally, letting his hand slip up between Jack's butt muscles, and of course down deep under the enormous stick and the bag of jewels, was a total mistake, —as Sammy tried to convince Jack with a laugh in his voice.

As Jack finished drying and getting re-dressed, he told Sammy. "Hey man. I'm going to leave my briefs here. I want to go back with everything hanging loose. You don't mind do you? Tell Jim why they are here as soon as he gets home so that he knows you and I did not do the ole cave exploring thing again. If he finds them, he'll think we did some of the getting down deep into the hole thing again."

"Hey, Jack. Jim wouldn't care, and besides he'd just be plain jealous if we did do it. He's already told me that I have his complete OK to get it with you just as often as I can, because he will be getting in your pants just as often as he can, too. We've pretty well agreed that if either one of us gets a chance with you, to just go for it. The three of us getting together is so hard to schedule, that we decided that whenever, just go for it. But, I will tell you, he is real anxious to play with you again, so if at all possible, try to save some time Friday afternoon since he'll be home early that day. OK?"

"Yeah, hell yeah! Hey, anytime that you guys know ahead of time when one or both of you will be available, always let me know. Like I told you! I've got to get my nuts off everyday, and I'm depending on you two to help me do that. Hey, Sammy, if I and this Mark guy do it, and we have some fun together, is it OK if I use you guys as a kind of a go between, if he wants to contact me? I don't think having him call my house is too good of an idea, and I know calling the apartment office too often would not work. Is it OK if I tell him to call you guys and have you two let me know when to stop by his place? Hey, this might turn out to be a good thing for you guys too. If that hunk starts playing around, maybe he would like to stop by here once in awhile too. Sammy, once you see him, you would be as hot to jump him into bed as I am right now. He is a hottie!"

Jack got the OK to give Mark their phone number if things worked out OK, and he then hit the door to head back toward Mark's apartment.

Jack knocked on the door, and Mark answered. Immediately, Jack realized that Mark had found enough time to apparently, not only, take his wife to work, but to also change clothes, too. Mark now had on a tight, very tight red tank top, and a pair of black, short, butt hugging, gym shorts. Jack, rather returned the earlier up and down looking, but this time from him to Mark, and he did not mind if Mark noticed him doing the looking. Mark looked hot, and Jack could not accept any other thought than, "Mark did this to turn me on. And it is working! Big time!"

"So did you get your wife to work, OK?" Jack asked.

"Yeah, sure did." Mark replied as he allowed Jack to enter, and then closed the front door, and— although he could not see, since he was in front of Mark, Jack rather thought he heard the door lock click. He smiled, even with just the idea of that happening, even if it had not actually happened. He enjoyed the idea that perhaps, Mark would lock the door behind them, meaning they were now in a locked apartment, just the two of them. Just the two men. One man that was ready to jump the bones of the resident, and the resident that Jack still did not know for sure all about. Hopes and dreams, yes, but true knowledge, he did not know.

"Which shower? The hall bathroom, or the bedroom bath?" Jack asked.

"Oh, it's the bedroom bath. Drips all the time."

As Jack headed down the hall, he inquired. "You just moved in, right?"

"Yeah, yes. We moved in about 2 weeks ago. Still trying to get everything all organized."

"Oh, OK!" Jack replied, and then wishing to continue the conversation so that Mark would stick close by, he continued. "So Mark. What type of work do you do?"

"Oh, I'm the new assistant coach over at Northside High. Haven't actually started working yet since school doesn't start till the 5th, but I finally got a coaching job. All the others have just been stuff like history and math teaching. Finally got what I've been wanting."

"Hey, —Great!" Jack exclaimed! "Congratulations man! I'm glad for you! That is great! What does your wife do? I guess she's got a job someplace already?"

"Yeah. She was lucky. She got a job at Smith Lumber in the HR department. That's one of the reasons we decided on this apartment complex. It's close to her, job, and like today, she could come home for lunch. Of course when I'm at school, she probably won't come home at noon so often, but for now it's kind of nice, and it saves some lunch money that way too."

Jack pondered the, "Mark took her back to work at 1:00 from lunch, that means she does not have her own transportation; Mark will need to pick her up from work; he took her back to work at 1:00, it is now no more than 10 after, and he got his clothes changed into some more tighter and sexy stuff since he got home, knowing that I would be here right away! Hmm!? Interesting, and I think—damn —I hope, —is playing right in my direction. Got to play this right!"

"So I guess instead of calling you Mark, calling you "Coach" is now more appropriate, right?" Jack asked as he smiled and looked toward Mark.

"Hey, that sounds so good! Hardly anybody has called me coach yet, so yeah, if you don't mind, I'd appreciate that. Yeah— Coach! Yeah, I like that! Maybe once school gets started more people will be calling me coach, and then maybe I'll get used to it, but yeah, today that does sound damn good to me. Thanks! Yeah, if you will, call me Coach. I need to kind of get used to it!"

"OK Coach, what will you be coaching?"

"Oh just about everything. You know Northside High is not a very big school, so they don't have a very big coaching staff, so as the assistant, I will actually be assistant to just about everything. But, hey, what the hell—people can finally call me "Coach." I'll do this for a couple of years, and then try to find something more like a head coach's spot, but for now it's not history and math."

"And hey, besides all coaches need to do their time taking care of the shower rooms, and keeping those guys in order, don't they?" Jack rather smirkingly asked, as he looked toward "Coach" to see how he took that remark.

Coach grinned and simply said, "Yeah, I guess," but as he said that, Jack saw him take one more, quick glance down toward Jack's crotch. Jack wondered if Coach had noticed that his manhood was now showing a nice firm rounded shape extending down his left leg, as it had not been earlier, when he was at the front door, and before he saw the hot body that he was going to be working so closely to.

Watching the Coach's expression as very closely as he could, Jack was certain that he did detect a change of expression as Coach glanced down. He was certain that Coach's eyes did open just a little wider as he focused in a little closer. Jack was hoping that the coach just might be getting a little turned on by what he was looking at! And he decided that if the coach was getting a little excited, he sure was gonna do whatever he needed to do, to keep the coach moving in the right direction!

Jack proceeded into the shower with some tools in hand to correct this major dripping problem that he was now so happy was happening, and Coach stayed in the bedroom putting some things away that still had not yet been un-boxed from the recent move.

All of a sudden Coach heard the running of water in the shower, and he heard Jack rather let out a disgusted yell of, "Oh crap! Oh shit!" and immediately the water was turned off. Once again Coach heard Jack exclaim. "Damn it! Crap!"

As Coach turned toward the bathroom, he saw Jack step out of the shower and rather shake his hands and his head. Coach went over to the bathroom to see what had happened. He knew from Jack's expressions that something had gone wrong.

"Shit man!" Jack said as Coach approached. "Damn man! Look at what in the hell I did! Damn it! I forgot that I had not turned the water supply off, and like a dumb shit, I turned the shower on. Coach, I am all wet. Hey, man. Would it be OK if I stripped down and used your dryer to dry these pants. Shit man, I can't go outside with them looking like this. It looks like I pissed my pants. You've got an apartment with a dryer in it don't you?"

Realizing that nothing extremely bad had happened, Coach rather started finding some humor in the happenings, and he replied, "Yeah, we've got a dryer, and yeah you do look like you just pissed in your pants. Here, take them off and I'll put 'em in the dryer. Your shirt is wet too. Take the stuff out of your pockets and give 'em to me. I'll get you a towel to use."

Coach turned to retrieve a bath towel from the hall closet and as he did, Jack looked up, watched him leave the bathroom area and smiled. He unbuttoned the shirt, and he quickly slid off his pants. As Coach re-entered with the towel, Jack stood there with no pants on, and his shirt completely unbuttoned. Coach, gasped! Jack looked at him, and asked, "You OK?"

"Oh yeah—yeah, I'm OK. Sorry, guess I was just kind of shocked when I came around the corner. Sorry!" Coach said as he handed Jack the towel.

"Shocked?" Jack asked. "Coach, what do you have to be shocked about? Didn't you expect me to be kind of naked here since I was taking off my shirt and pants? I mean, you did expect me to take them off, didn't you?"

"Yeah Jack. Yeah I did, but," he attempted to say as he looked at Jack's stripped body, "But, I'm sorry Jack, —Jack I don't know. I did not quite expect to see that, I guess."

"Expect to see, —what? My dick? Coach, we're both men. You knew I had a dick, didn't you? I mean, you are a coach, you know guys have those things!" Jack rather laughingly asked, as he looked rather slyly at Coach's crotch and noticed that his gym shorts were now tighter fitting than they had been when he entered the apartment.

"Yeah, Jack, yeah. I guess I expected you to have some shorts on, I guess. I'm sorry, I just got kind of shocked when I came around that corner. I did not expect to see you all naked there. And shit man! I've been around a lot of naked guys before, but shit man, I've never seen one quite like that! My God Jack, that damn thing is enormous!"

"OK so you saw me, well, —see me, all naked now. Am I OK? You are a coach; you probably should be able to tell if a guy is built right or not—right?"

Taking a big deep breath, Coach managed to say, "Yeah, yeah— you are built right! God Jack! You are, —what should I say, you are built more "right" than any other guy I've ever seen. Shit Jack, I'm sorry, but that damn thing really is shocking when you don't expect it! Jack you are one damn hot built man! Oh shit Jack, I'm starting to say stuff that I probably should not be saying. Jack, you have got one God of a body! Jack, I'm sorry, I hope I'm not making too much of a fool out of myself, but man—oh Jack! I've never told another guy he is hot, or ever said anything about his dick, but shit man, when I saw you at the front door earlier today, I damn near fell over. And that was before I saw that thing! Jack, you are one hot and well built man! Oh shit man-I'm making a fool out of myself!"

"OK, so you say you have never told another guy he is hot, but I'll bet some guy has told you before that you are hot, hasn't he?

Come on Coach, some guy has told you before that you are a hottie, hasn't he?"

"Well, yeah, once. Yeah, a guy did once, but I kind of told him to go find a girl."

"Did you find him kind of hot, or was he all bad? How did it feel to be told you are a hottie?"

"Jack, I'm not gay. That guy was wanting to feel me. Yeah, he was nice, but he was trying to grab ahold of me. We were in the YMCA shower, taking a shower."

"So did he grab you?" Jack asked, as he noticed that without him even being aware of it, Coach was getting a pretty good boner. He realized that as tight as Coach's shorts already were, that if he got any stiffer, there was no way in hell that Coach could avoid knowing it much longer. The boner was secretly giving Jack the unspoken, 'go-ahead,' that he was so damn glad to see.

"Yeah, he did for a second or two. I moved away from him, though."

"So what did it feel like to have him holding you? Did it feel OK to you?"

As Jack was asking Coach about being handled, Coach looked down and after seeing that Jack's rod was standing out stiff, he took a very deep breath, kept his eyes on Jack's mahogany stick and said very quietly, "Yeah, it felt good! Yeah, Jack, I liked him grabbing it, but I knew he was not supposed to be doing that. I made him let loose, but I knew I really didn't want him to! I was kind of mad at me later, for making him let loose."

"Coach, I like to be grabbed, too. You're looking at it, —grab it for me, —please. Take ahold of if, please!"

Without so much as a word, Coach reached out with his left hand and put it on top of Jack's cock. He grabbed ahold of it, attempting to wrap his hand around it. Continuing to watch what he was doing with Jack's cock, he then reached up and placed his right hand on Jack's left pec. Slowly he leaned toward Jack. He squeezed the black rod, and he rubbed tenderly the chest muscle. He leaned forward toward Jack and placed his lips on Jack's chest. He rested his head against the mass of chest muscles. He quietly asked, "Oh God Jack! Oh God what am I doing? Oh Jack, Oh shit! You feel so good to me! Oh Jack, is this OK that I feel you? Oh Jack, please don't be mad at me for feeling you. Oh Jack, I don't know you, but Oh Jack, — I love you! Oh man! I've wanted to feel somebody like you for so long now. Oh Jack is this OK if I feel you?"

Without saying anything, Jack moved Coach back about three steps and laid him down backwards on the bed.

"Oh Jack, Jack, I'm married. Jack I can't do this, I'm married!

"So am I!" Jack softly and quietly said, as he laid across Coach.

Hearing that, Coach immediately grabbed ahold of Jack and buried his face in the nap of Jack's neck. He slightly kissed him. "Oh Jack, I'm so fucking scared shitless, but Jack I want to do this! Squeeze me please!"

Quietly without talking, Jack and Coach silently slid around on each other, feeling each other's skin and gently kissing each other in all manner of ways and in all manner of places. Jack allowed Coach to remain clothed, but did not let the shorts nor the tank top from keeping him from feeling all of the body parts that he wanted to get his hands on. Although it was still confined inside of the gym shorts, Jack could tell that Coach possessed the appropriate type of a cock shaft that every coach should have. He could tell that as the years went on, once one of them got a chance to see it, his athletes would find good opportunities to talk about how well their coach was hung. He knew that Coach was going to be a coach talked about whenever the student athletes needed something sexy and exciting to talk about. He knew that a lot of students have fantasizes about having sex with their coach, and Mark was going to be the subject of many dreams.

Finally, Coach quietly whispered, "Oh Jack. Jack, I can't believe this is actually happening. Jack, I have never played with a guy before, nor had a guy hug me like this and I've wanted this for years. Jack, I've never been loved like this before! Jack, get me naked so I can feel all of you with my whole body. Please take my clothes off of me, please!"

With those instructions and requests, Jack removed Coach's tank top and his gym shorts and his black, sexy jock strap. It was not a school issue jock strap! It was a special, mail order, type. A type not usually available in local stores. Much more of a type used for photo sessions, by hot, sexy, models! He leaned his face down toward the now escaped dick, and he kissed it. He felt it jump as Coach felt Jack's lips touch it.

"You like that?" Jack asked. "Did your dick like getting kissed?"

Coach grabbed ahold of Jack tighter, and kind of muttered a, "Yes."

Both men were tightly in the hold of the other man, but neither seemed to have much attention directed toward the two stiff dicks that they constantly needed to reach down and slightly move out of the way so that they could continue their licking and kissing. Each man knew this was really turning out to be more of a loving session, rather than just a man on man sex session.

"Oh Jack, I've never felt this before. Jack, let me feel you all over me. Jack you are so fucking hot man, you are so damn hot!"

"Coach, you are hot too. I knew when I was here before you took your wife to work, that I just had to get you. I knew then I wanted to feel you. I love your dick. Coach, you are going to be one hot coach, man! Coach, —I kind of guess you have never fucked some guy's ass before,—right?"

"Oh Jack, No —no, —I've never fucked a guy's ass. Jack until right now, I've never even laid down with a guy before, but I've known for a long time that I really did want to, and when I saw you at the door, I knew I would probably loose my control today. Jack you are so damn hot, and yes,— I will admit it, whenever I dreamt about getting together with some guy, someday, I always had this dream that it would be some hot looking muscular black man, and when I saw you, I knew I was finally going to live my dream. Jack, if you had not wanted to do this, I would have cried for days. I want to try and see if

I can put your dick in my mouth. Oh God! Oh shit! I've been trying to say that ever since we laid down here. Oh shit! I can't believe I finally said that! Jack, I can't believe how much guts it took to just say that! I mean, I'm here in bed with you, and I was so damn scared to just say that! Oh Jack, I've wanted to do this for so long. Oh shit, man, let me see if I can put my mouth on it!"

Jack moved himself and Coach both so that Coach was in a good position to try and see if he actually had enough nerve to try and suck on Jack's dick. Thinking that maybe Coach needed some encouragement to actually do it, Jack reached down, grabbed ahold of Coach's dick and immediately went down on it completely.

"Oh God! Oh God! Oh God that feels so damn good!" Coach almost screamed! Jack sucked and made sure that Coach could get a good strong feeling of what getting a good manly blow job felt like. He pulled Coach up tight to his face. He swallowed all of Coach's dick. He estimated that Coach was swinging about eight and a half or nine inches of a nice, very nicely thick dick. As Jack ate more and more of Coach's dick, Coach slowly and very nervously placed the tip of Jack's strong dick at the edge of his lips. Jack watched, but decided to let Coach take it at his own pace. He did not want to scare him out of taking it. Coach slid his lips over the tip. He tried to force his mouth down on it farther. He took deep breaths through his nose. Jack knew that Coach was doing something that he had dreamt about doing for years, but even though he now had the chance to do it, he was about to have a heart attack from the fear of actually putting some guy's dick in his mouth. Jack slowly put his hands on Coach's head and softly encouraged him to attempt as much cock into his mouth as possible. Coach could only manage about one half of the length.

"Shit man!" Coach exclaimed as he pulled off of it. "Damn man! I knew you had a big dick when I saw you the first thing earlier but shit man, I had no idea you had that much. You have got one hell of a big dick. I can not believe that now that I actually have a man's dick in my mouth, that it is one this big! Shit, I should have started with a smaller one. Jack, I'm sorry I can't take all of it. The way you have been sucking on my dick and taking all of it feels so good, I wish

I could take all of yours that way. I'm sorry I just can't get that much in my mouth. Hell, once I thought it was going to make me throw up! Jack, you have got one hell of dick! Jack, God man! Did that dick just grow that way, or did you do something to it to make it that big?"

"Hey man! For being the first time, you did one hell of a good job! You took quite a bit of it. Got to tell you, most guys don't take that much. You suck good. Real good for your first time too. You'll get used to it. We'll keep working on it!"

"Jack, how often do you get with some guy? You said most guys can't take it very well. Do you play with guys a lot?"

Jack explained about how he needs to do some good gay sex almost everyday, and so yeah,—he plays with as many guys as possible, and how he was hoping that Coach could become one of his regulars.

After the explanation, Jack immediately slammed his face back down on Coach's dick, and very quickly sucked him to a very high excitement. He let Coach have some dick action that was completely new to him. As Jack pumped on and off of Coach's dick, he sucked on it probably with a little more suck than he has used on any guy lately. He knew that when Coach let it fly, that cum would be his first with a guy sucking on his dick, and he wanted Coach to be damn glad he had done it, and maybe regret that it had taken him so long to finally get a good male sucking. As Jack worked it, he heard Coach getting excited. Jack was handling Coach all over. He wanted Coach to feel the complete and total experience of having a man on him, and eager to take part of him. As he sucked, he kept grunting "Yeah man!, Yeah man!" He knew Coach was about ready to let it fly, and he knew that he had to be ready. He could tell that if he did not have his face firmly planted on that dick, that as excited as Coach was getting, when he climaxed, the cum would fly completely across the room and make spots on the wall. He knew he had to be the dam to catch the flow.

Suddenly Coach started yelling, "I'm going to cum! I'm going to cum! Oh shit Jack, I'm going to cum!"

Jack uttered back at him, "OK, OK" and attempted to rather shake his head "yes" to encourage Coach to let it fly. "Yeah, Yeah,"

Jack muttered and he grabbed ahold of Coach and pulled him up tight against his face.

It hit! It flew! Jack got a mouth full! Coach grabbed ahold of Jack's head and locked himself to it. He pushed and forced his entire dick into Jack's mouth as firmly as he could. He kept fucking Jack's face, although he was not actually getting any motion other than forcing his dick and Jack's head back and forth.

"Oh shit man! Oh Jack, Oh God Jack, I came! Oh shit man,—I think I drained all of me in you. Oh God Jack, was I supposed to cum in your mouth? I did not know that I was going to cum. I don't know if I was supposed to cum in your mouth.

As Jack continued to lick his lips and make sure that he was swallowing all of Coach's cum, and not letting any of it escape, he told Coach that he had done exactly what he was supposed to do. He filled his mouth and throat with his warm man juices, and that is what Jack had wanted. Jack and Coach both collapsed and hugged each other.

Jack had gotten a good mouth full, but his nuts needed to be relieved, and he was still supporting an enormous hard-on.

"Hey Coach, I've got to let my load fly. I've got to let my nuts get some relief. I'm going to jack myself off, and you can help if you want."

Coach reached over and took ahold of the big rod that he had tried to get in his mouth. He jerked on it with one hand, then he grabbed ahold of it with both hands and gave it a great time. Rather quickly Jack reached down and rather breathlessly said, "Oh, Coach. Let me do it, I'm getting close! Oh yeah! Oh let me spray you. Can I spray you?"

Moving without waiting for an answer, Jack quickly rose up and positioned himself above Coach's chest and let fly. If Coach had not wanted a chest full of man sperm, it was way to fast for him to complain. Jack raised up, and all of a sudden the cum was coming. Five big strong loads, loads largest enough to match the size of the cock they were flying out of, and Coach had been baptized with his first spraying of another man's juices.

Jack rolled over on his back and apologized to Coach. "I'm sorry. Maybe I should not have done that to you. I hope that was OK. I should have asked you if I could cum on you. You OK?"

"Yeah, hell yes! I'm OK!" Coach replied. "Shit man, what a fucking load. Hell man, when I cum, it would take me probably four of five climaxes to unload that much juice. Jack, I can see why you have to get your load off every day. Hell if you didn't, your bag would be the size of a basketball!"

Jack then told him, that maybe not this day, since they had already been playing around for quite some time, and they had now both just cum, but soon, very soon, he wanted to see if he could fuck Coach's ass, and would the coach let him do that? "Coach, I want to shoot a load up in you so that I know you and I are really connected together. Can I try to fuck your ass sometime, real soon?"

Expressing his absolute fear, Coach did admit that the idea of getting a dick up in his ass, has been one of the dreams that he was dreamed about for years, but he had some really big doubts about getting that much stuck up in his ass. He told Jack that he had some real fears about getting that much meat stuck up in his ass, but after watching him shoot his big hot load all over his chest, the idea of getting that shot up in his ass was getting him all excited. He said that until just then, he had never thought about getting a hot load shot up in him, but now he had something new to dream about. He knew he wanted to feel a hot load hit up inside of him, but he was real scared about how that much dick up in his ass would feel. He reminded Jack that he had not even been fucked with a little dick yet. A big one like he has? Scary! Damn scary!

Jack reassured him that it was completely possible, and told him to talk to Sam in apartment 117 if he wanted to talk to someone that has already taken it, to just find out from a taker, how it feels once it is up in there. He told Coach that he knew Sam would give him a good straight, honest, and probably an excited, answer.

Coach wanted to hear more about this Sam guy, and as they laid there and re-cooped, Jack told him about how he was new at the apartment complex, how he had met Sam and then later Jim, and how

Sam had told him that they would be the go-between if Jack and Coach needed some vehicle of contact since they were both married guys, and could not be calling each other directly. Jack also told him, that he thought perhaps Sammy and Jim might be some additional good partners for him, if he had decided that he might like some additional action.

Coach expressed his rather warm feeling toward that idea, and admitted that now that he has had his first gay experience, he was anxious to meet Sam and Jim. He admitted that now that he had finally broken though the big barrier, he knew he was going to want to find other playmates. Then Jack told him that if he wants to meet more gays, he had moved into the right complex. He then told Coach that was the reason he took this job when it finally came open. He told Coach that this complex had more gays living in it than any other apartment complex in the area. And, he continued, "Once the word gets around that you are a coach, watch out! A lot of guys will be wanting to meet you! And do more than just meet you!"

All of a sudden, the two men realized that Jack's wet shirt and pants had never been put in the dryer. Coach grabbed them up, and headed for the washer and dryer.

After Coach returned from putting them in the dryer, he asked Jack what he was going to do about the shower leak, since that little project had gotten interrupted.

Jack explained, "It actually had not been interrupted. The faucet had been completely fixed before I turned the water on myself, making it look like that had been a big stupid mistake. I actually did that on purpose, so that I would have a good, wet, reason to take my pants off. My little act worked, didn't it?"

CHAPTER FOUR:

Want Some of This?

"Hey, Sammy. Hi! Hey, is Jim home yet?" Jack asked as Sammy answered the phone.

"No Jack, but I expect him any minute now. Are you on your way?"

"No Sammy. I've got to stop by apartment 139 and fix a falling closet rod. A Greg and Susan, somebody, —can't remember their last name right now, live there. I can't find out anything about them other than that they've been there for about a year. Do you know them? You know anything about Greg that I might want to know before I get there?" Jack asked.

"Hey Jack. All I know is that I've seen them come and go a few times, and I've always been disappointed that she was always with him whenever I saw him. I'm sure he probably would have no interest in me, but I'd sure love to get a chance to know him. He's hot looking, well to me anyway."

"Oh really?" Jack replied. "How? What does he look like?"

"Oh I'd say he is probably about 24 or 25 years old, about 6 foot tall, real dark black flat top hair cut, and obviously a guy that belongs to a gym someplace. I've seen him without a shirt on, and he's got a great six pack gut. Nice butt, but that's about all I can tell you. One of those hot looking straight married guys, that get gay guys like me all turned on, and then they go off with their women and let me stand there all huffing and puffing wishing I could just reach out and grab ahold of him."

"Oh hey good! Hey, maybe fixing the closet rod will be more fun than I had expected. I didn't know anything about who they were and I couldn't find out anything from in the office file, well other than that they moved in here about a year ago. Hey Sammy, I'm going to run over there and take care of that, and then I will be over to your place. OK?"

"Yeah Jack. Jim should be home right away, and I know damn well he will be here as soon as possible because he knows you won't have too much time available tonight and he wants to make the most of what time you do have. We'll be ready for you when you get here!"

"OK guy. I'll be there shortly. Get the ole grease can out and get your ass ready! I've been anxious for it all day! I'll see you guys shortly!"

Jack hung up the phone and headed for apartment number 139.

Jack knocked on the door. He waited for a moment and then was greeted by Susan. Entering the apartment he was then also greeted by Greg and immediately agreed with Sammy's statements about how hot this guy was. After a few casual introductory comments, Greg then showed Jack to the main bedroom closet where the clothes rod had actually come loose from the wall and had fallen. All of the clothes that were supposed to be hanging there were neatly stacked on the floor.

"Oh great!" Jack exclaimed to Greg as he saw what had happened.

"Yeah!" Greg replied. "Opened the door yesterday evening, and everything was on the floor. I guess it fell sometime while we were gone. Made kind of a mess."

"Yeah I sure could see where it might have." Jack said as he rather stood there and looked at where the rod was supposed to be, at the stack of clothes on the floor, and as he got a chance, at Greg's basket and his muscular chest that was very pronounced under his tight T-shirt. Greg saw him looking. Greg grinned, and Jack did the same. Jack definitely got the feeling that getting checked out was not a problem to Greg.

"So I guess you must work out in a gym someplace, right Greg? I mean man, you've done good for yourself."

"Yeah Jack I do. I am the assistant manager of the Roosevelt Street Athletic Club. You obviously have worked out a hell of a lot too haven't you?"

Jack shook his head "Yes," and took another look at Greg. Greg appreciated it. He flexed his biceps in the same way that a little boy does when he wants to show off his arm muscles. Jack grinned, and following, what he was hoping was an invitation to do so, he reached up and placed his right hand on Greg's left tight bicep.

"Nice, real nice man!" Greg said. As he did, he once again looked over Greg's torso and again said, "Nice, real nice man!"

Greg replied, "Thanks, and coming from you, I really do mean a big thanks!" As he looked Jack over and then reached forward and felt one of Jack's upper arms, he continued, "I'd love to give you a free month's pass to come work out at the club. I think you would be good for business. Fact is, I'll be right back! I'm going to get one and give it to you. I'll get one and be right back."

Greg left the bedroom and went back into the living room area. Jack opened his tool box and pulled out some tools and screws to start working on the closet rod. He heard Greg say to Susan, "Hey honey, I'll be back here in the bedroom seeing if I can help this maintenance guy out any."

47

Greg returned and instead of handing Jack the gym pass, he slid it into Jack's hip pocket, and rather pushed it down in far enough to make sure it did not fall out. Jack realized that he had just been given a little more than a gym pass. As Greg pulled his hand out of Jack's pocket, Jack looked at him and let out a big grin. Greg replied with one of his own.

"Hey Greg. I'm having some trouble getting this thing to stay in place while I try and re-screw it to the wall. Would you mind getting in here and kind of holding it in place for me?"

"Sure, yeah I can do that. What do you want me to do?"

"Here Greg, why don't you get in here, hold this in place and I'll reach over you to fix it."

Greg stepped into the closet as Jack moved to the side to allow him some room to move past him, and as he moved in, Jack then stepped back into place and allowed himself to rather lay up against Greg. Greg looked at Jack and grinned. Jack raised his eyebrows in a very playful and encouraging manner. He then said very softly, "Yeah! Yeah!" and wetting his lips, again grinned at Greg. He shook his head up and down softly.

Greg caught on! He looked down at Jack's crotch area, and Jack again said, "Yeah, yeah! If you want to, it's OK."

Greg took a big deep breath, looked at Jack's face and uttered a "Wow! Can I? Really?"

"Yeah, you're hidden. I'll keep my eyes open. I want you to do it!"

Greg reached down and grabbed Jack's crotch. He pushed his body up against Jack's. Jack grabbed Greg's crotch and as he did he continued to make comments about trying to get the closet rod to stay in place as if he was still actively working on it, instead of working on Greg. Greg kept a very nervous eye open looking through the crack of the door hinge to make sure Susan was not walking into the bedroom. He looked up at Jack and silently smiled and then pulled his hand up so that he could rub Jack's chest. Very softly, very softly he said, "Oh shit man! Oh shit! I work at a gym, but I never get to do this there. Oh man! Shit this is fun!"

The two men continued their mutual feeling session as long as Jack felt they could safely get away with it. Greg was obviously very nervous. Jack knew that Greg was very excited about being able to do this, but he also knew that Greg was scared shitless about the possibility of Susan walking in and seeing what was happening in their bedroom.

Jack then looked at Greg, put on a big grin, and rather loudly asked, "Greg, have you got anymore closet rods that you think might need to be fixed so that they don't fall?"

Greg replied. "Yeah, I think maybe we need to look at this one in the other bedroom and fix it, if you have the time."

Shaking his head as if to say, "Good going man," Jack did reply, "OK! Let's fix it too."

Greg and Jack went into the other bedroom and Greg removed everything from off of the closet rod. He placed it all on the bed. He then said, "I'll help you with this one too, if you want."

"Yeah, if you will," Jack replied. Both men knew that everything they were saying was for the benefit of Susan, and to allow Greg the opportunity of getting in the closet's tight quarters, in the pretext of helping Jack, when of course, in reality, it was to feel Jack and let Jack feel him.

Just as Greg was getting finished in removing everything from the closet rod, he then yelled to Susan, "Hey, honey! I didn't stop at the mail box and get the mail today. Since I'm helping this maintenance guy with these closet rods, would you mind running up and getting the mail before it gets dark outside?"

Susan told Greg that she'd do that, and that she would be right back. She left the apartment, and as the door was heard snapping shut, Greg immediately turned to Jack and had him in his hands and was feeling all of Jack's strong, muscular, and tight, body.

"Oh Man! Oh Jack, I almost shit when I came in the room and saw you when you got here. Oh God Jack, I hope it's OK if I feel you! Jack is this OK? Oh Jack, I've wanted to do this to so many of the hot looking guys in the gym but of course you know I can't do it."

"Yeah Greg, yeah man, it's OK. Greg you know damn well why I "needed" your help in the closet. I thought maybe you needed a reason to get up close and tight, and I knew we couldn't be seen in there. How long will she be gone to get the mail?"

"Oh probably no more than 5 or 6 minutes if she comes right back. Oh Jack, I've never played with another guy, but man, of all of the guys that come to the gym, I've wanted to for so long! Oh shit man! I know damn well I should not be doing this, but man I guess I just couldn't help myself! Jack, how can we get together someplace? I mean, you will play with me won't you? Jack, do you play with guys or am I making a complete stupid fool out of myself here?"

"Yeah Greg, I play with guys, and no, —hell no man, —you are not making a fool out of yourself. You are one hot hunk of a guy! Yeah, we will play. Greg, you know damn well us guys need to have all kinds of sex fun. We need to use each other whenever possible. You've worked on that body of yours and made it pretty great, so now it's time to let someone like me enjoy it. Greg, I'm married too, so we need to do some planning here. Jim and Sammy down at apartment 117 are some playmates of mine. They don't mind if I kind of use them as a go-between when some guy wants to contact me, so I'll write their number on the back of the work order sheet that I leave with you, —so don't ask what that number is when I hand it to you. Their names are Jim and Sam. I told Sam that I had to come here to work on a rod and he told me that he has only seen you, never actually met you, but he told me that you are one hot hunk. I'm going over there right after I leave here, we've got ourselves a little play session planned for tonight, and I'll tell them what's happening. Maybe we can ask them if we can meet in their apartment sometime. They're good guys. They might be a good teacher for you too if you want."

"Oh God man! Oh shit!" Greg exclaimed. "I can't believe I'm doing this. I can't believe it, but damn it man, I've known for years now that I wanted something like this to happen. So what do I do? Just call that Jim and Sam and let them handle getting us together somehow?"

"Yeah, I'll fill them in. If you can find any way possible, to get out of here for a few private minutes later after I leave, come to number 117 and we will be able to talk more. We had better get onto this rod before your wife comes back and realizes we haven't done anything since she left."

"Yeah, but man, we did a hell of a lot more, since she left, than what you realize. Oh Jack, I'm so damn excited about finally getting close to getting with some guy. This will all be a big secret, right?"

"Oh hell yes Greg! Yeah man! I'm married too! Yeah, we have to keep it a secret, but Sam and Jim will help us. Just make sure you call them as soon as possible if you can't get out of here for a few minutes tonight. OK?"

"Yeah, I will. I'll see if I can find a reason to get out of here after awhile though. They won't mind if I stop in there?"

"No they're cool. I'm sure they are going to be real glad to help both you and me out!"

Jack and Greg resumed their "in the closet" positions, and as Jack did put in a couple of new screws to re-enforce the closet rod, they continued to feel each other up as if the other man was his personal toy. Silently they groped and rubbed. Greg slid his hand down along the shaft of meat that was hanging down Jack's left pants leg, and he reached around with both hands and squeezed Jack's butt muscles. When he felt the size of Jack's meat stick, he looked up at Jack and said, "Oh God man! Is that all you?" Jack just shook his head, "Yes."

Jack had his left hand on the back of Greg's neck, and his right hand on Greg's now, getting stiff, cock. He rubbed it, then told Greg that maybe he had better stop that or Greg would have to explain to Susan, when she got back, of why he was supporting a major boner. They heard the front door open, each man rather straightened himself up some, and Jack immediately, and rather loudly asked, "OK that one is fixed. Greg, are there anymore that need to be fixed?"

"No, I think that should take care of all of them," Greg replied, as he grinned and winked at Jack. He reached over to Jack and squeezed his hand as he just mouthed, "Thank you man!"

Jack re-gathered his tools and Greg replaced the clothing that he had taken off of the closet rod. Jack took out his work order pad and wrote quick notes as to what type of work had been done, turned it over and wrote the number 117 and Jim and Sam's phone number on it, folded it and gave it to Greg, simply telling him that was his copy. "Just office paperwork. Just so we can keep track of what repairs I do, I guess!" Jack said as he handed the folded paper to Greg.

Greg put the paper in his shirt pocket.

Jack picked up his tool box, Greg extended his thank-you's for doing the repairs and followed Jack to the door. Jack told Susan, "Good-bye", turned to Greg and told him to call the office if there was anything else that he needed done. He then shook Greg's hand and as he went out the door, he said, "See you later!" Greg slowly shut the door.

Jack arrived at Sammy and Jim's apartment, and as he entered he carried a very large grin.

"OK man! What's up?" Sammy asked as he looked at the big grin on Jack's face. "What happened man?"

Jack told Sammy and Jim about his episode with Greg and how turned on it got him. He told them in great detail about how Greg has never been with a guy before, but as the assistant manager at the health club how he has wanted to play with a guy, but never could. Jack told them that he had given Greg their name, apartment number and their phone number so that they would have some way to stay in contact with each other. He told them about Greg's body. He let them know that from what he had felt, Greg was swinging a pretty good-sized rod of his own. They laughed about what had been going on in Greg and Susan's bedroom closet while Susan was still there. They then agreed on how chancy gay guys will get, whenever they get it in their heads that they simply have to do some fun stuff with another guy.

As the three talked about Greg's new experiences, they realized that this whole conversation definitely did have a very humorous twist to it, since it all happened over a "rod in a closet".

Jack said, "Yeah, come to think about it, there was more than one rod involved, and Greg was more physically in the closet than just figuratively speaking. Well, maybe that little closet session will help him out of the closet!"

Jack told the two that Greg said he was going to "try" and come by the apartment, if possible, so they decided that they needed to do their playing around is such a manner so that if the door bell rang, one of them would be able to quickly grab a pair of pants and go answer the door.

The men moved themselves to the bedroom, undressed, and each played with, and licked and rubbed the nicely exposed parts of body that were not normally displayed while clothed. Jim and Sammy definitely took advantage of having Jack standing completely nude in their bedroom.

Jim kneeled down in front of Jack, and acted as if Jack's entire body was covered with honey that needed to be licked off. He grabbed ahold of Jack's legs and slowly and deliberately ran his mouth and tongue up one side of one leg and back down that leg before he then repeated the same process on the other leg. Crossing from one leg over to the other, he lifted Jack's hanging ball sack with the top of his head, and with his head pushing up in the crotch of Jack's hot black body, he reached out with his tongue and slightly licked the super soft skin between Jack's sweet ass hole, and his "family jewelry" bag.

Sammy stood behind Jack, and reaching up as far as he could since Jack was quite taller than he was, he licked the muscular back, up one side of it, down the other and then slowly and very lovingly up the middle of Jack's back, so that he could feel Jack's thick back muscles touch the sides of his face as he slowly moved up toward Jack's neck. Reaching the base of his neck, Sammy then moved his tongue along Jack's right shoulder and continued down the entire length of his right arm. Reaching his finger tips, Sammy slowly took each finger into his mouth and sucked on it. After completing each finger, and the love made to it, Sammy then moved himself back up Jack's right arm, across his shoulders and then proceeded down his left arm. Once again, as he got to Jack's hand, he worshipped each finger with his mouth and then returned up the length of his arm, licking the underside of Jack's arm as he went.

As Jack was being worshipped from the front and from the back, he stood there as if he was the dessert of the day, to be eaten and enjoyed by any person that was lucky enough to get some of that delicious dessert placed on his plate. Without interrupting either man and his actions, Jack would softly place his hand on some part of Jim or Sammy's body to let each of them know that he was in complete glory being treated in this manner. He realized that he had become the common item of attention between two lovers, and that he just happened to be the item of choice for them to share as an increasing part of their personal relationship with each other. He did not look at this as so much as a sex session for himself, but rather as allowing himself to be used by these two lovers, and being used as their common goal for the day. Silently as he stood there and allowed the complete exploring and sharing of his body, he realized that at that moment he was not actually a human being, but was actually much more like a tall dark doggie that the two owners were sharing their love for. At one moment he even, without actually intending to do it, let out a small groan, as if he was a puppy getting some very warm loving and petting from his two owners.

As he groaned, Jim looked up at him in question. He knew something was happening but he did not know what. He wanted to be sure that everything was OK with Jack, and that neither one of them was doing anything wrong. Jack realized that he had made that verbal sound, and he just looked back down at Jim and mouthed, "Wow" to let him understand the groan was a good groan, not a bad feeling.

As Jack looked down and indicated that everything was OK, Jim pulled his head back from being so close to Jack's legs and placed his mouth on the tip of the 11 inch rod sticking out in front, at such an attention. He placed both hands on the cock and steadied it so that he could attempt to put as much of it in his mouth as possible.

Just as he opened his mouth and pulled on Jack's cock to join the two together, the front doorbell rang.

Sammy immediately jumped up and said, "I'll get it. Keep it up guys!"

Sammy grabbed a bathrobe that was laying across a bedroom chair and headed for the front door. Shortly he returned, with Greg beside him, and they watched for a few moments as Jim forced himself onto the outer one half of Jack's rod.

Jack looked over toward Greg and Sammy and nodded a "Hello." He then grinned at Greg as he looked down at Jim sucking on his dick, and then looked back at Greg as if to ask, "Want some of this?"

"Keep it up men!" Sammy said. "Greg, the one with the mouthful is Jim, my other half. Of course you already know Jack, but maybe you are now getting a chance to meet more of Jack than you did earlier."

"Oh God!" Greg exclaimed. "Oh my God Sammy! Oh shit man! I did not know his dick was that damn big! Oh shit man! Shit man! Do you guys actually suck on that whole thing?"

"Hey Greg, we do as much as we can! I've been fucked by it, and I think Jim is going to try and take it tonight. Right Jim? You are going to try and take it up your little ole tight ass hole, aren't you?"

Without removing himself from the rod, Jim looked over toward Sammy and kind of shook his head, "Yeah". Then he uttered a mumbled, "I hope!"

Greg and Sammy stood there for a few more moments and watched Jim attempt another three or four more inches into his mouth, when Greg told the others that he only had a couple of minutes before he had to leave, but he sure did want to figure out how he could get together with them before he had to get back to his place.

"I told Susan that I wanted to drive past the gym to see how many cars were there to see how busy they were, while she was working on some sewing that she was involved in. I hope nobody saw me get in the car, drive around to this other parking lot and then get back out again. I had to move the car in fear that she could come out for some reason and see it sitting there. Then when I got over here, I could not find your number 117. Damn, the numbering of these apartments is a mess. I finally found it, obviously, but I was getting really worried that I couldn't."

The sucking stopped for a few minutes, Jim and Greg met, and more comments were exchanged about the bodies that both Jack and Greg had, and could so proudly show off, and they discussed the necessity of secrecy, about knowing each other, since both Jack and Greg were married guys, and the additional fact that Greg lived in the apartment complex.

Since Greg worked mostly night hours at the club, as the assistant manager he explained, that is the joy of being the assistant, he said that if at all possible trying to get together some morning before noon would work best for him. Susan worked at a retail store as a buyer and she was always gone in the mornings. Sammy explained that since he was a teacher and school was still out for the summer, he could make it anytime. Jim said that since he was off on Monday's and Tuesday's, one of those mornings would work for him. Then he looked at Jack and asked, "Jack, can you do a morning somehow?"

"Yeah I can. I've got to work some night hours shortly so that I can work on that leak in the laundry room when nobody is using it, so let's decide what day will work for you guys, and I will tell the office that I'm going to be working at night, on that day."

After slightly more discussion, and of course some crotch grabbing, especially from Greg, the one that had never grabbed a man's cock before, they decided that Tuesday morning at 9AM would work for everybody. The plans were made for Greg and Jack to show up, back there, at apartment 117, bright and early at 9AM on Tuesday morning, and Jim and Sammy would have some homemade breakfast rolls ready for all of them to dive into.

Jim and Sammy also agreed that they would have the "extra room" all set for some good actions, as Jim put it, "Just in-case we decide that two beds are better than one!"

Greg complained rather vocally about how pissed he was that he had to go, how he was really horny and was really wanting to get started then, and not have to wait until Tuesday, but he was glad that they had been able to get plans set up. He told everybody to have fun, as he looked down at Jack's big boner again, shook his head in disbelief, and then left.

"Hey, one hot guy!" Jim pronounced as Greg left the apartment. "So, he has never done anything with a guy before?" He asked as he looked at Jack.

"Hey he told me this evening that he has always wanted to, and he has known for quite awhile now that he was wanting to play with a guy, but he said he never has. He got all excited when we were playing with each other in the closet. I really do think he is totally new to this. Anxious, but new! I think I know why he is working at the club. He got that job because he knew, or maybe subconsciously knew, that he would be around hot and sometimes naked guys. You know people do that stuff without actually knowing why they are doing it. He's admitted that he's been wanting something like this to happen for a long time now. He told me today that when I came into his apartment, he knew he was going to loose it! And I kind of guess he did! He's the one that stuck his hand down in my back pocket and gave my ass a grope and a feel, by putting that gym pass in there. When he did that, I knew he was asking for it! Hey, —like I always say, —if you are hot, you don't have to ask twice!"

"OK, then." Jim said. "I've only got enough guts to ask for it once. Are you going to try and get in my ass?"

"Try!?" Jack rather quickly and excitedly asked. "Try,—hell no! I'm not going to "try", I am going to fuck you all the way, and you are going to beg for more! Get in there and get your ass ready, my dick is hungry for some good ole tight ass muscles to grab ahold of it!"

With that comment, the three men returned to the bedroom, and Jim laid down on his stomach, ass in the air, and asked Sammy to sit up by his head so that he could put his face in Sammy's crotch, while he, as he put it, "Loose my ass. Shit man, I have to be completely out of my mind to agree to this!"

With Sammy in place under Jim's face, Jim belly down on the bed, and Jack now poised above him, dick in hand, he smeared some grease on his one third of a yard long dick, and a good amount up into Jim's ass.

"I put some grease up in your ass man, but I really did that just so I could feel up in your butt." Jack said. "I can tell your ass is not going to be nearly as tight on my dick as you have been saying it would be. You are used to getting stuff stuck up in there aren't you?" Jack asked.

"No, not really." Jim answered. "Yeah, I get fucked once in awhile, but nothing like your dick. Why, does my ass feel open or something?"

"Well, let's just say, it sure is anxious for something to go up in there. I almost had my whole hand up in you while I was greasing you up. Your ass is hungry man! Real hungry!"

With that statement, Jack aimed the tip of his enormous rod right at the opening of Jim's back side, and slowly, but firmly guided it in. Jim jerked. He bit Sammy's crotch hair. He rather slightly let out a yell of, "Ouch!"

Sammy asked him if he was OK. He shook his head "Yes".

Jim grabbed ahold of Sammy's waist and pulled himself forward and buried his face farther into Sammy's crotch. He said, "Sammy, tell him to push in a little more."

Sammy looked at Jack to see if he had heard the comment, and Jack indicated that he had. He lowered his torso, and part of the big 11 inch dick, down into Jim a little farther. Jim moaned and indicated that everything was OK. He then uttered, "Yeah, more! Do it again!"

Jack again lowered himself down and pushed more of his mahogany rod on into Jim's ass, some more. He pushed his rod into Jim's ass as he listened to hear anything that Jim might say. All he heard was the repeated, "Yeah, more! Yeah, more!"

Jack looked up at Sammy and said, "He is really taking it. He is getting an ass full pretty damn quickly back here. I said his ass was hungry! Man, I'm going in him faster than I did with you. I thought you were supposed to be the one with the hungry ass. His ass is eating my dick as fast as I can give it to him!"

"Good!" Sammy replied.

Jim laid there taking more dick, both in length and in girth, than he had ever taken up into his ass before, and he was listening to what sounded like a radio report on how this guy was getting it in the ass, and how fast he was taking it. With Jack's report to Sammy, he felt as if maybe he was not expected to hear what was being said, but was to just lay there and be the subject of attention. He grinned. He thought his mental process was really kind of funny. My ass, he is in my ass, he is laying on top of me, all of his body is touching me, inside and out, but at the same time, he is talking as if I'm not even here. I'm a "piece of meat"! I am a "piece of meat" to him right now! This is what they always talk about being a "piece of meat!"

Jim did not mind his feelings, —like he was only a "piece of meat". He rather liked it. This was turning him on! He knew he was being used, and he was being used by one very hot, handsome, built, strong muscle man, that just also happened to have an 11 inch, very thick and meaty dick on him, that was now, all the way up inside of himself! He smiled! He knew he was being used like some animal out in a field, getting a rough fucking by another wild animal. He felt wild, and he liked it! He was another "piece of meat"! He did not feel like he belonged to himself any longer. He felt like he now completely belonged to the man that had so completely taken over his entire being, by putting so much of himself up inside of his body. He felt that his body had been totally overtaken by this other human being! He felt that they had become "one". He then loudly, forcefully and almost yelling, said, "Fuck me,—Fuck me! Fucccccck me!"

Sammy and Jack both were quite surprised at Jim's very vocal instructions to fuck him. They both understood immediately that Jim did not mean,— "kind of fuck me," they both knew he truly meant that he wanted it in the ass like he had never had it in the ass before!

"Yeah man! Fuck my ass! Let me feel you up in there! Fuck me! Fuck me! Fuck me hard!" Jim was almost yelling his instructions to fuck him, and to fuck him hard!

Sammy looked at Jack, Jack looked at Sammy, and he then truly went to work on Jim's ass. Jack was in complete surprise that Jim wanted it that roughly. Sammy was in shock! Jim was yelling, "Fuck me! Fuck me! Fuck me hard man! Fuck me hard man!" Jack was fucking his ass as hard as he possibly could! He was slamming it! He was exhausting himself trying to fuck Jim as roughly and as forcefully as he was asking for!

Jack suddenly found out that he had a man, under him, that was one hell of a lot more of an excited, hungry assed guy, than he expected to be fucking that night. He gave Jim everything that he asked for. Jack looked up at Sammy and in-between humps and ass slamming rams, he told Sammy, "I feel like some wild fucking bull out in the field! Man, I had no idea your Jim was this damn wild! Shit man, I have not been yelled at to fuck some guy's ass like he's been doing,—for a hell of a long time! Shit man! I really don't remember ever having been yelled at like that to fuck some guy's ass! Especially when it was his own ass and not some other guy's ass!"

Jim rather jokingly said, "Shut the hell up, and fuck me! Fuck me!" Then he actually did yell out, "Fuck me!"

Sammy looked at Jack and rather laughed, but at the same time had somewhat of a look of confusion on his face. He had never heard Jim get that vocal about getting it in the ass.

Jack looked at Sammy and laughed back, and then attempted to ram all of himself into Jim's ass. "Shit man! He wants more than just my dick up in there, I sure can see that!" Jack said to Sammy as he fucked Jim's butt hole faster and rougher than any hole he had been in for a long time. "Shit man, I hope like hell he can walk tomorrow. I'm not sure I'm going to be able to!"

Suddenly as he was commenting on the possibility of not being able to walk tomorrow, Jack got a funny look on his face and grabbed a hold of Jim's body and started yelling that he was getting real ready to cum.

"Oh shit man! Oh shit,—I'm cumin! Oh man, I'm cumin! Jim, I'm going to load you man! Oh hell man, here it comes! I'm cumin, I'm cumin!"

Jim grabbed a hold of Sammy and squeezed him. Jim moaned and again grabbed a hold of his lover. "Oh shit man! Oh Sammy he's loading my ass with juices. Sammy I can feel all of his cum up in me! Oh Sammy he just fucked the hell out of me didn't he, Sammy?

Sammy, Honey, —I took his dick. I took all of it didn't I? I got all of his dick up in me, didn't I? Sammy he fucked me didn't he?"

"Uhhh, yeah Honey, he fucked you! Yeah, you got fucked! You got fucked big time man! Honey, you kept yelling at him to fuck you! You OK? Honey, you really kept wanting more and more and more! You OK?"

"Oh yeah, I'm OK" Jim rather exhaustedly answered. "Oh shit man, I'm tired. Oh Honey, he fucked me with all of his dick, didn't he? He had it all up in me, didn't he? Did he have all of it up in me?"

"Yeah Honey, yes, he had all of it up in you. You kept begging for more, and you kept yelling to fuck you harder! Jim, Honey, you do remember yelling to fuck you harder, don't you?"

Jim rather rolled over as far as he could, since Jack was still plugged into his ass, looked up at Sammy and he very exhaustedly asked, "I did? I kept yelling for him to fuck me harder? Sammy did I really do that?"

With every concern in his voice that a person can have, Sammy answered, "Yeah Honey. Yes you did! Don't you remember telling him to put more up in you and to fuck you harder? Jim, don't you remember telling him to do that? Honey, don't you remember telling him to shut up and fuck you?"

"Oh Honey, no I don't. No, I don't! Honey I got so excited once he got it up in me, I just don't remember too much Honey, I just remember that I did want to feel it farther up in me, and then I do remember getting all excited, but I don't remember yelling to fuck me or telling him to push it in farther, or anything about shutting up and fucking me. Oh Honey! It felt so good up in there that I guess I just got all too excited. I'm OK, but I guess I just got too excited and did not really know what I was yelling for! Hey, Honey, don't worry, I'm OK. I feel good. I'm OK. I don't hurt. I'm really OK!"

"Shit man! Shit man!" Was just about all Jack could manage to say. "Jim, you mean to tell me that all the time you kept yelling at me to fuck you harder, to fuck you harder, you really did not know you were begging for it? Shit man, I've had a hell of a lot of guys beg for me to get it out of them, but I do have to admit that you are the first guy that yelled for more of it and he didn't even know he was begging for it! And to think that just a few minutes ago, you were all scared shitless that I was going to hurt you if I stuck it up in you. Hell man,— I've never had this happen before! Jim, you did something tonight that I have never had happen before. Man, all I can say is you are one madman when you get fucked! When I told you your ass was hungry, I sure as the hell did not know I meant that damn hungry! All I can say right now is that the next time I fuck you, I will make sure I have taken a good long nap and rested up before I get on you again! Shit man! I'm usually the one that wears the other guys out! Tonight, you whipped the hell out of me! What a fuck you are! What a fuck!"

CHAPTER FIVE:

Don't Let That Scare You

Tuesday morning arrived, as did Jack and then Greg, only about five minutes after Jack arrived.

"Hey Greg, come on in man." Jim invited, when he saw Greg approaching and as he opened the door for the now rather popular Apartment 117.

"Oh man! Got to tell you guys I'm really nervous about this!" Greg said, as he entered the apartment and joined the other three men at the coffee counter.

"Hey, Hi Greg! Hey man, everything is going to be OK!" Jack encouraged. Come over here and get a roll. Sammy is one great cook! These are delicious!"

As Greg came around the edge of the counter to join Jack as he had suggested, suddenly Greg realized that although Jack still had a T-Shirt on, he was sitting at the counter completely, and totally, bare assed! From the shirt bottom on down, it was all beautiful bare mahogany, slick, and lickable skin. A sudden sight that would take any person's breath away.

"Oh shit man!" Greg exclaimed as he saw the very, very unexpected view. "Shit man! I just told you guys how nervous I am about doing this, and now I walk around the counter and find this big long body part hanging out here all bare and showing. Shit man! Do I really know what I am doing? Oh shit man, that fucker is just too fucking big! Look at how long it is and look how fucking thick it is! Oh my God man, that thing looks like it belongs on a fucking horse of something. Oh shit man, do I know what in the hell I'm doing?"

"Hell yes you do man!" Jack encouraged as he reached out and placed his arm around Greg's shoulder and neck. "Greg, my man. The night I was over at your place, fixing those clothes rods, you were ready to jump me, —there and then, —so just remember how excited you were that night, and I'm sure you will get over being nervous now. None of us are going to do anything to you that makes you uncomfortable. So everything is going to be OK! OK?"

"Yeah I know!" Greg answered. "I know when I started out from our place, to come down here, I told myself then, that I just want to have some good man-to-man sex, and that I just need to get rid of this nervous thing, —since I'm finally getting a chance to do it!"

Then looking over at Jack, and then down at Jack's now half hard dick, Greg pleaded, "Jack, please tell me that you won't do anything with that big thing that I don't think I can do. OK? Please, man, that dick of yours is so damn big! I really can't imagine anybody being able to get fucked by it."

"Hey Greg," Sammy entered. "Greg, don't worry! Seriously everything is going to be OK. We know today is your first time doing this, so whatever you want to do, or not want to do, is OK with us."

Greg again looked down toward Jack's massive rod and then asked. "Hey guys. Can maybe I play with one that is a little smaller than that one until I get convinced that I can play with a bigger one? I mean man! Shit, that pole is so damn big!"

As Greg talked about it, and kept looking at it, Jack's rod continued to get harder and harder.

"Shit man!" Greg strongly said. "God man! Jack make it stop getting bigger and bigger. My God man! The bigger it keeps getting the more scared I am of even being in the same room with it! Jack, weren't you scared that you were gonna tear up the insides of the first guy you ever fucked? Weren't you really scared that damn big thing could really rip up a guy?"

"Well Greg, gotta tell you, —no! See the very first time I ever poked this thing up in the backside of some guy, he was damn near screaming for it! I was, oh I think maybe 19 and I was on my way to Memphis to go visit my sister. I was on route 40, someplace between Memphis and Nashville, in some little coffee shop that was part of a motel. I'd eaten my dinner and was in the restroom. I'd taken my piss and I guess, —that when I got done, I was a little too slow tucking it away. Some guy, found out his name was Larry, was in the process of washing his hands, and also, watching me through the mirror. When I kinda turned partway around, but hadn't tucked all of it inside yet, he flipped around and said, 'Oh shit man, oh my god! Oh man alive! Oh man let me see that thing!' He came right over to me, and yes, —he actually grabbed ahold of it right as I was tucking it away, and he pulled it back out! He stood there and kept feeling it and looking at it! Well, yeah, up until then I'd never had some other guy feeling my dick like that and yeah, it started getting hard! I was shocked! I really didn't know what to do! Here I am, in a restroom with some guy, that yeah, —he was pretty damn good looking, pretty well built and looked all kinda taken care of, and he's rubbing my dick and making it get hard! I was fucking afraid somebody else was gonna come in, but man, if they had, there was no way in hell I was gonna be able to get my woody back in my pants!"

"Anyway, he told me that he just had to get fucked by that dick, and he wasn't kidding! He didn't say it in any kind of a funny way, he was serious! He told me that he needed it, and he needed it bad! Then he asked me if I'd ever fucked some guy with it, and of course I told him "No!" That's when he asked me if I was on the road by myself, and of course, I did tell him, "Yeah, just me."

"He told me he had a room there in the motel and that he was gonna make it well worth my while to come to his room and get my first piece of guy ass, that I'd ever had."

"Now I'm standing there with a major, major hard on! I guess all eleven inches of it was sticking out by that time. He bent over and licked the end of it and told me again, 'See, I'm serious man! I'll make it well worth your while to come to my room and do it.' He opened up his billfold, showed me two fifty dollar bills and said, 'You do it, —those are yours!'"

"Hey men, —I was poor, —well still am, but back in those days, a hundred bucks was gonna go one hell of a long way for me! That was gonna more than pay for my trip to go see Sis. I said, 'Okay, I'll do it!' Did not know what in the hell I was in for, how this was all gonna happen, but hey, for a hundred bucks, I was willing to learn!"

"We left the restroom and headed for his room. We got inside and the door no more got closed and he had his hands all over my crotch! He grabbed me like he was afraid I was gonna run away. He started getting me all undressed, —that was the first time a guy had ever done that to me, and then he got all undressed too. Gotta admit, he was hot! Thank goodness, cause for a hundred bucks, I was gonna be fucking this guy's ass, and right then, I will admit, it was starting to look pretty damn good! I think he was maybe 35 or 36, about six foot one or two, light brown hair, probably maybe about 190 or 195 and a dick on him too! For some white guy, he was hung. But then, you gotta remember, since that was my first time knowing that I was gonna be doing some funny stuff with a guy, it might have looked bigger than it really was. He got all undressed, he grabbed something like some KY or something out of his toiletry bag, rubbed some on his ass, some on my dick, leaned over, grabbed ahold of the dresser and said, "Fuck it man, fuck it!"

"I asked him, 'Ain't this gonna hurt man, —ain't it gonna hurt?' He kinda looked back at me and said, 'No, no. No man! Believe me man, it ain't gonna hurt me any, just put it in me, —fuck me! Come on guy, fuck me! Fuck me now!'"

"Okay my first time up and inside of some guy's ass, —I went in! He told me to fuck him, and I did! Yes, I did! I got that damn thing up in him, and I found out how fucking good it is to have my dick up inside of some guy's ass, and I fucked the hell out of him! I grabbed ahold of him around the waist, I pushed in on him, and I pulled back on him, all at the same time! He shook the hell out of that dresser he was holding onto! The mirror on it I thought was gonna fall off! It shook like hell! For probably ten minutes I pounded his ass so fucking hard that I was sure he was gonna scream in pain, but he never did! All he ever said was, 'Fuck me man, —fuck me! Harder man, —harder!'"

"Now of course I'd never shot off inside of some guy before, and all of a sudden I decided that I was just about to let something fly, and I tried to ask him if I needed to pull out, and all he could say was something like, 'Hell no man! Hell no! Fill me, fill me!' or anyway something like that! So I did! Yes I did! My first climax inside of some guy's ass, he got his one hundred dollars worth! If he could have gotten pregnant I think after that he would have had probably about two dozen little guys! I fucked him hard, and I loaded him good. So anyway, that was my first time fucking a guy's ass, and yeah, I found out right away, it ain't gonna tear up some guy's ass by poking it up in there! Hell, even trying to fuck him like I was a jack hammer, didn't do him any wrong! So from that time on, if it's there and available, I take it!"

"So Jack," Jimmy asked, "Did you get the hundred bucks?"

"Oh yeah I did, and guess what! He told me that if I'd stay with him that night, that I didn't have to pay anything for the room, and I could fuck him some more if I wanted. But not for money this time! I was planning on driving some more, before just sleeping in my car, but yeah, I stayed, and yeah, I fucked! Probably three more times that night! I learned fast what to do when it's available!"

Greg once again looked down at Jack's stiff rod, and said, God man! That guy had to have been fucked a lot before he ever saw you and that damn big thing! He must have been trying to find the biggest dick around, —and then decided he had! Damn I would have thought that kind of fucking back there had to have hurt him some! Jack, —if you end up fucking me, you gotta go a lot easier on me than you did on him, okay? Gotta remember, I've never been fucked before, never!"

Jack patted Greg on the head and assured him that he would! "You'll be okay man, you'll be okay. I'll take care of you, I will!"

"Hey Greg. Tell you what!" Sammy said. "After we get done in here and then head for the bedroom, why don't you and I start with each other, and we'll let Jack and Jim screw around with each other. Then after you can kind of get into it a little more, then if you want to play around with Jack's dick, then you can. I kind of think that if you watch Jack play with Jim again, then you'll remember how excited that was the other night when we watched Jim suck on him. Everything is going to be OK, and you are going to be real glad that you finally got a chance to do it with a guy. I sure can tell you that once I found out that you were going to be coming down here to our place, that sure turned me on. I've eyeballed you ever since you and your wife moved in, and I've been wanting to play with you ever since. So trust me, we are all going to have some fun. Good fun, —good gay fun!"

All four men enjoyed some additional conversation and the rest of the home made breakfast rolls when Jack stood up and taking hold of Jim's arm, he politely said, "Sorry guys,—but I did not come here just for some talking! I'm horny and I need some ass. And from that I heard earlier Jim, I kind of guess it is your ass that I get. Well, that I get first, anyway. Right?"

Jim immediately got up and followed Jack down the hall, slapping his bare ass with each step, and chance that he got, until they got to the master bedroom.

As they entered the bedroom, Jack finished getting undressed, and Jim of course immediately stripped nude. Looking at Jack's bod, Jim again took a very big sigh and said, "Man, I just have never seen a hotter, hot and tight body like yours before! Damn Jack, you are so damn hot! I am so glad Sammy and I got the chance to meet you, and better yet, get to play with you! Get that dick good and stiff, my ass has been yelling for that thing ever since you fucked me the other night! Damn, that big rod feels so damn good all the way up in me."

Jim laid down on the bed as he watched Jack pull his T-Shirt off over his head, and then reach down and give his "Jack-stick," (as Jim had found out Jack liked to call it) a few strokes, when Jim told him to get it good and stiff. Looking at Jim, Jack then asked, "Is that stiff enough man? You want this?"

"Oh fuck yes I do man! Yes Jack, put some jelly on it and put it up in my butt! Please, fuck me real hard again!"

Jim laid down on his stomach and rather kept pumping his bare ass up and down as if to be begging with it, for Jack to get that enormous rod of his up and in there, as quickly as possible.

Jack lubed up his rod, and after carefully placing himself right above Jim's ass, he aimed his rod, placed the tip of it at the opening of Jim's ass, and then asked Jim if he wanted a nice slow entry, —to get the ole asshole opened up slowly, or did Jim want to take it all at once.

"Oh Jack! Ram me! Jack I want to know that I can take that whole damn thing up in me as quickly as possible. I want you up in me, and I want you up in there all the way! All of you all at once man, yeah I wanna feel you go up in me! Please put it in me man, —please!"

"OK man!" Jack replied. "Remember you told me you wanted it all at once, right? You still want me to just ram you?"

"Yeah, yeah, please just ram me!"

"Hang on! Here I come!"

And with that final statement, Jack filled Jim's ass with every bit of the eleven inch dick that he had! Length and width, it all went in, and it went in immediately!

Jim yelled in pain! "Oh my God Jack! Oh my God Jack, Oh My God, that hurts man! Oh shit man, —Oh God my ass! Oh Jack! Oh Jack, — oh my ass!"

Jack immediately stopped moving on Jim, and just laid himself down on Jim. "Hey man, you told me you wanted it like that! You OK? Jim, you OK? You told me to just ram you!"

"Oh yeah I know Jack, I know! I know, I told you to do that, and I guess I forgot how damn big that thing is when it's up in me. I'm OK, I'll be OK, just lay there for a minute and let my ass quit hurting! Oh man! Oh Jack, I get so damn anxious and so damn horny for you and that damn dick of yours, I forget how damn big that thing is! I forgot that you've got a fucking baseball bat for a dick! It feels like it's the same fucking size and I damn well know, your dick is just as hard as some wooden baseball bat! I'm OK Jack, just lay there a minute!"

As Jim and Jack were laying there, letting Jim recover, Greg and Sammy came into the room. Sammy looked at Jack and asked, "He told you to ram him all at once, didn't he?"

Jack looked at Sammy and answered that, "Yeah he did. He told me that he wanted me to just get it all up in him as fast as possible, and that he just wanted me to ram him. I guess I've got to quit listening to him when he's all horny like that and says that!"

"When I heard him let out that scream, I knew exactly what had happened. He told me earlier this morning that he wanted you to slam your rod up in him as fast as possible and I told him then that he had better think about that. I tried to remind him about how damn big that rod of yours is, but all he could say is that he knew it was big, but he wanted you to ram his ass as hard and as deep as you could the first time you go in. I swear, for a guy that hardly ever got it in the ass before, he sure goes crazy with rage when he gets fucked by you, Jack. Shit man, I wonder just how much dick could he take up in there!'

Jim then turned his head to the side and looked at Sammy, said, "But Hon, it feels so damn good once it is up in there! I know, I need to just have him work it up into me a little slower, but shit, when I know that dick is up there aimed at my butt, I want it, and I want it all at once. I know, I scream when it hurts, but it must be a good hurt, cause now it feels so good! Hey Jack, I'm OK, fuck me! Let me feel you up in me!"

Sammy turned and looking at Greg said, "Hey man. Don't let that scare you. Jim is just so damn anxious to get that whole big rod of Jack's up in him as fast as he can, he takes it way too fast! He forgets that Jack's big rod is not some feather duster, getting pushed up in there! I've been fucked by Jack and that pole of his, and believe me man, it feels good! If you let Jack, or for that matter, any guy go up in you kind of slow, and get your ass opened up a little slower, it feels good! Come on, let's you and me go in this other bedroom and start doing some good stuff and let those two go at it for awhile."

Sammy and Greg did go into the extra bedroom and started touching each other and getting down to some good gay man business.

"You OK?" Sammy asked of Greg as he threw his T-Shirt over on the chair and lowered his shorts to let his manhood fall free.

"Yeah I'm OK, I guess. Just nervous as hell, though! Sam, I've wanted to do this with some guy for years and years now, but now that I'm getting all undressed, and you are standing there all bare and naked and with a hard on, I'm nervous. I don't know how long you've been playing with guys, but were you this nervous the first time you did it?"

"Yes Greg, yes. I'm sure all guys are nervous the first time they finally get together with another guy. And to be honest, I do kind of think that the older you are when you finally get started, the more nervous you are. You're OK. I'll only do whatever you want, so you have complete control. OK?"

"Yeah thanks Sam, I appreciate that!"

"OK Greg, your instructions! What do you want me to do? You tell me what you want."

"Oh God Sam, I don't know. Can maybe we get started with you kind of playing with my dick? Maybe jerk on me or something?"

"Oh course we can do that Greg, you stand there and just put your hands on my shoulders. You just let me play with your dick, OK?"

Greg stood there with his stiff rod sticking straight out, and Sam knelt down in front of it. Greg put his hands on Sam's shoulders as Sam had suggested, and after putting his hand around it for only a moment or two, Sam then leaned forward and after opening his mouth wide, he slid his mouth onto Greg's dick.

"Oh my God!" Greg let out. "Oh my God! Oh God Sam, —you have my cock in your mouth! Oh Sam, I never thought this would ever happen to me! Oh God Sam, suck on me! Yeah, let me feel you on my dick! Oh God Sam, that feels so good! Oh Sam, I have wanted some guy to do this to me ever since I was in junior high and saw it happen to another guy. Oh Sam, yeah—please, please suck me man! Please suck on me man, suck on me!"

Sam turned Greg sideways and gently lowered him back down onto the bed so that Greg was now laying down, and Sam was on top of him, with Greg's entire dick stuffed down his mouth.

After just resting there for a moment or two without moving any, Sam then started some true action on Greg's cock rod, and started Greg's first, true cock sucking. Sam was going on and off of that stick with all of the gusto that he could manage!

"Oh my God Sam! Oh Sam that feels so good! Oh you are making me so hard! Oh Sam my dick is getting so hard it almost hurts! Sam I'm not sure it's ever been that hard before!"

Sam used his experiences, to give Greg one unbelievable sucking, that Sam simply wanted to know, Greg would look back at with very fond and enjoyable memories.

Greg quickly caught on that to grab hold of Sam's head and to use it as a jerk off tool, gave him some control over being able to push his dick as far down into Sam's throat as possible. Sam had Greg's dick in his mouth, and his balls in his hand. As he played with the dick in his mouth, he also played with the balls in his hand. Greg was truly being given, a physical treatment that he had never experienced before.

Each time that Sam went down onto Greg's rod, he grabbed ahold of his bag a little stronger and then each time he came back off of it some, he loosened the grip. He could tell from Greg's reaction that Greg was truly enjoying both the mouth action, and the grip action. He kept letting out moans and groans of acceptance. He kept slightly saying, "Oh thanks, oh thanks! Thank you man, thank you! Oh man, this is so good, —this is so good!"

Sam was not even sure that Greg was aware that he was uttering the 'thank you's.' Listening very closely, Sam decided that Greg was just barely on the edge of reality and the most of him was off into some other outer zone of bliss and pleasure! Someplace that he had never experienced before!

As Sam continued to work on Greg's rod and grabbed his bag of balls, he also ran his hand up between the cheeks of Greg's butt, and up toward Greg's sweet little ass hole. Greg let out an almost scream that, "Oh Sam, I'm about to cum! Sam, I'm going to cum! Oh Sam, please, I'm about to cum!"

Sam understood that Greg thought that Sam would want to get off of his dick, when he knew that Greg was ready to shoot his load, but Sam tried to let Greg know that he did not want to take his mouth off of it! That he wanted to take Greg's cum load down his throat as it flew, and that Sam wanted to be hugging Greg as firmly as he could as Greg shot his wad!

"Oh God Sam, I'm cumin man, I'm cumin! I'm about to cum!"

Suddenly Greg raised the mid section of his body, let it get totally stiff and rigid and then really yelled out, "Oh God Sam, I'm cumin man, oh God man, —I'm cummmmmin!"

Greg's body and his dick got extremely stiff! No part of him moved, except for the steady flow of cum that he shot out of the end of his dick. His dick was thicker and harder right then, than he had ever felt it to be before! He felt each large and small squirt of cum as it left its shoot rod! He knew he was feeling this climax much more, much more, than any other time, regardless if it had been while having sex with his wife or some other gal, or even when he jerked of. He knew, even the very first time he ever jerked off, it had never felt this good and this exciting! He felt like his whole body was exploding just like the Fourth of July fireworks! He just felt like everything around him was exploding, and exploding in a very big way! He wanted to reach out and grab it! He wanted to hug it, and kiss it, and hang onto it! He loved it, and he did not want it to stop!

Sam pulled Greg up as close and as tightly to his mouth as he could, so that he did not loose any of Greg's, first time, gay load. He felt Greg expel his man juices, four strong and powerful times. Each time, Greg let out a very loud, "Oh Man! Oh Man!" And then a final, "Oh shit man! Oh God that felt so damn good! Oh man! Oh God that felt good! Oh God that felt so fucking good!"

Sam continued to keep his mouth tightly sealed onto Greg's dick, and continued to suck the very last drop of the man cream out of Greg's dick, before he then slowly slid off of the dick, looked up at Greg, smiled and then asked, "You OK man! You OK?"

Greg laid there completely exhausted, looked down at Sam and tried to confirm that he was OK, but he was breathless and could hardly talk. He managed to smile and utter something like, "Yeah, I'm OK, I'm great! Oh man, I can't believe it man, I can't! I finally did it, I finally did! I knew it was gonna feel good, but I sure as hell did not expect it to feel that fucking good! Oh shit man, —that was better than having straight sex, —a hell of a lot better! I don't think I've ever shot off that hard before! I don't! I don't! Thanks man! Thanks!"

CHAPTER SIX:

One Small Step at a Time

Sam and Greg remained stretched out across the bed as Greg attempted to rather regroup himself, and slowly accept the true fact that he had just been completely blown by another man, in another man's bed, and now he was laying there hugging that man, feeling that man's bare skin up against his own bare skin, and was truly relishing in the joy of knowing that the same kind care and treatment was being returned back to him, from his — he could not believe it, — his male, —sex-mate.

"Oh Sam! Sam, I never knew letting a cum load fly, could feel that damn good! Sam, I know I shot harder and stronger that time, than I ever have in my entire life. Oh Man! What a great feeling that was!"

"Greg, I hope it was great for you because I know that no man ever forgets the very first time that he gets his rocks off in some other guy's mouth. I knew that I had just one chance to make your first blow job a winner right then, and I was trying to give you everything I could give you so that you would always remember this blow job with the greatest of memories and maybe always classify it as one of your very best!"

"Oh shit Sam, I kind of think it will always be way up there as one of the best! Damn man! How in the hell did you learn to suck some guy off like that? I'm sure you didn't suck on some guy like that the very first time you did somebody, did you?"

"Oh, hell no Greg! Shit no! A guy kind of lives and learns with each time. He just tries to make himself that much better each time he does it, and hey—like they say—practice makes perfect. And I love to practice!"

"God Sam, all I can say right now is that you sure have had your amount of practice then, because you sure as hell know how to suck a guy off! Sam, if I get into sucking on guys, do you think I will ever be able to do it like that, or have I, kind of, gone past my prime time when I could really learn how to do it that good?"

"Hey Greg, my man! It's never too late! I'm sure some of the world's best cock suckers never got started until they were a little older, and shit man, you sure as hell are not an older guy yet! Just because you didn't start sucking cock when you were younger sure as hell does not mean you will never learn how now!"

Then as Sam finished that statement, he did notice that Greg was looking at Sam's hard rod with what looked like a rather strong amount of interest, as if he was thinking about something.

Sam softly asked, "Greg, want to try it? It's there man, it's all up to you."

"Oh crap man!" Greg almost exploded. "Oh shit man! Sam,— I know damn well in my heart that, yes I want to, I've wanted to for a hell of a long time now, but shit man, sucking on some other guy's cock?! Sam, I have always been taught that is just something that only the "funny kind of people" do. Sam, it has been beat into my head that doing something like that is really perverted and sick. God man! It felt so damn good when you were on me, and I've wanted to know for so damn long what it would be like to do something like that, but shit man, all that crap they teach you as a kid is really hard to get rid of. Shit man, oh Sam, yeah—yeah I want to, but what if I just can't do it? If I try and then freak out and can't suck on it, you won't be mad will you? I don't want to make you mad, but shit Sam, putting some guy's dick in my mouth is really, really kind of freaky!"

Sam calmly laid there and softly touched and rubbed Greg's chest and his upper leg. Every once in awhile, Sam would "allow" his hand to gently touch Greg's hard-on, just as a little jester to subconsciously keep Greg all hot and bothered inside, without him actually knowing that Sam was just silently keeping him all warm, anxious and excited to do the unthinkable thing!

Slowly Sam took Greg's left hand in his hand, and slowly placed it on his own hard-on so that Greg was making actual contact with Sam's stiff rod. Sam decided that one small step at a time was the cautious way that Greg needed right now. He knew, in fact, that Greg had said many times already that yes, he does want to suck a cock, but all of his childhood teachings were causing him some real mental problems. Sam decided to let Greg accept this act of passion, one small step at a time, and Sam was confident that if he let Greg do it his way, that Greg would finally do the "naughty".

Sam laid there and watched Greg keep looking at Sam's rod and watched Greg's tongue unconsciously slip out and wet his lip as Greg keep looking at Sam's cock, and tried to convince himself that putting his mouth down on it was doing the right thing.

Sam slowly maneuvered himself in the bed so that Greg's hand on his dick was very comfortable for Greg to reach, and also so that his dick was in a very acceptable position for when Greg did finally decided to put his face down on it.

Taking deep breaths and continuing to keep his eyes on Sam's cock, Greg kept telling himself that putting his mouth on Sam's cock was not going to be the worst thing that has ever happened in his life, and that he knew he had been wanting to do this to some guy, for years. He didn't say anything to Sam. Sam didn't say anything to Greg. Both men were completely silent for different reasons. Greg was totally silent due to the fact that his mind was completely overtaken with his mental war of telling him that it is totally wrong to put some guy's cock in his mouth, and it was even wrong to maybe give some other guy a kiss, and the other side of that war, that kept saying, "Yes do it! You want to do it, you've wanted to suck on some guy's cock for years now. You've looked a pictures of nude guys and have wanted to taste their dicks, but they were just pictures! This is a real man! This is a real dick and it is waiting on you to put your mouth on it! Now is your chance! You have a man here that is going to let you suck on him! You are in bed with him! His dick is right there, it is hard! It is standing right up in front of your face, you finally have a chance to do it, and to do it with a guy that is waiting for you to do it! Suck it man, suck on it!"

Suddenly, to Sam's surprise, Greg bent down and without saying anything, he put the tip of Sam's cock in his mouth. Just as soon as he did that, he pulled back off of it and said, "Oh God Sam, Oh shit, I think I did it! Oh Sam, I kind of did it!"

"Yes, Greg, yes you did. Not so bad was it? Your mouth didn't seal shut or your tongue fall out, did it? Are you glad you did that?"

"Oh yeah Sam! Yeah I am. Sam I'm going to do it again and try to put more of your dick in my mouth. Is that OK? Can I try? Oh Sam, I am so fucking nervous doing this! Sam, I never thought I'd ever get to do something like this with some guy. I knew other guys do it, but Sam, I really never expected me to get a chance to do it. Oh Sam, can I try and get more of you in my mouth? Oh Sam, I want to, can I?"

"Of course you can Greg. Hell yes man! That is why we are here! I'll just lay here and you do it again and try to put as much in your mouth, as you can. Do whatever you want to man! I'm just laying here letting you do whatever you want. I know you've wanted to do something like this with some guy for a long time now, so just take you time and do whatever you want. I'm not going to tell you to stop. There's no rush Greg. Take your time! Just do whatever you want!"

Greg looked up at Sam and just said, "Thanks man." He then pointed Sam's stick up directly toward his face and again he opened his mouth and kind of slowly slid his mouth down and onto Sam's rod.

Sam did not say anything. He simply, gently and slowly, rubbed Greg's shoulder so that Greg knew everything he was doing was OK!

Greg took a big deep breath through his nose, as he slowly slid his mouth down onto Sam's man meat. Slowly he let his tongue slide around the shaft as he started to do some actual sucking on Sam's dick, and slowly kept pushing his face up closer and closer to Sam's body as he managed to take more and more of Sam's cock into his mouth.

Sam could tell that Greg was almost beyond words for nervousness in finally getting to do this, but he could also quickly tell that Greg's terrible fear of doing this was rapidly passing as Greg took more and more of his dick down into his throat and more freely started expressing his joy, of having Sam's dick pushed into the back of his throat. Sam could tell that Greg was now starting to really get into this dick sucking stuff, as Sam could feel Greg doing some pretty strong sucking on his dick. Greg was definitely loosing his fear of having some other guy's dick stuck in his mouth! And stuck in his mouth completely!

Greg continued to use Sam's stick to his new and profound pleasure. Greg forced as much dick down his throat as he possibly could, and Sam could feel him forcing his mouth down onto his dick as far as he possibly could go! Greg then pulled off of it, looked up at Sam and said, "Shit man! Damn Sam, that thing feels so damn good stuck down in my throat as far as I can get it. It kind of chokes me some when I get it way down in there, but you know, I think that is part of the excitement of sucking on it! Sam, I am actually sucking on some other guy's cock! Oh Sam, I hate to tell you how many years I have dreamt about getting to do this with some guy! Sam, I am so damn mad at myself now, mad that I never did this with a guy a long time ago. You've got a damn nice dick, but now that I know I can suck dick, and I guess it's kind of obvious that I like sucking dick, now I'm getting real anxious to just see how much of Jack's dick I can get in my mouth. You've sucked him before, right? Is his fun? Sam thanks, damn it, for letting me do this. I am so damn glad you guys let me come over here! Oh Sam, I can't believe that this is the very first time I've even played with some guy, and now I'm getting anxious to see how much of that great big black dick I can swallow! Sam, am I weird or something for admitting that I want to play with Jack and that rod of his, so soon after just getting started?"

"Hell no man! You sure are not weird! You are smart! You know what you want and you are smart enough to admit it! Greg, there are countless number of guys out there that want a chance to play with something like Jack is hanging, but they are not smart enough to admit it to themselves. So,—consequently they never get to. You've seen it, you want it, and just because it's going to happen on the very same day of your fist gay sex, sure does not mean that you should pass up a great opportunity. Let's face it man! That is why Jim and I have both you and Jack over here today! We are both anxious to watch you and Jack get it on together for the first time. Hey,-when you two do get together, it is OK if Jim and I are in the room, —right? I mean, —I hope! We both want to be in there and maybe help walk you though that first time. I want to watch him fuck you!"

Greg looked up at Sam and just said, "Oh fuck shit man! Oh God Sam, his big dick up in my ass? Oh God Sam! Oh shit I don't know! It is so damn big!"

"Hey Greg, I know! But believe me, it's been up in my ass and if it didn't feel so damn good up in there, there is no way I would be encouraging you to get it! Greg, you've wanted something like that for a hell of a long time now! Don't let this opportunity slip by. Seriously man, you didn't think you could suck on some other guy's dick either, and now you are admitting that you like it, so getting a semi-truck driven up in your ass just might turn out the same!"

Then, just as suddenly as he came up off of Sam's dick, he immediately went back down on it and started sucking even stronger than he had been doing earlier. Sam was actually having some trouble believing that this was Greg's first time on a guy's dick. He knew that his comments about getting Jack's semi-truck driven up into his ass was getting Greg all excited and getting back down onto Sam's dick was his way of enjoying that excitement. Sam knew that as Greg was working on his dick, he was also imagining what it might be like, to be stretched out on the bed, having Jack positioned right up above him, right above his hungry ass, and so slowly, nice and slowly, starting his entry up into Greg's virgin ass. He felt that he could almost hear Greg thinking about getting it in the ass with that enormous rod!

"Shit man!" Sam said as encouragement but yet in some surprise to Greg. "Shit man! I guess when a guy doesn't start sucking dick until he's been thinking about it for a few years, then he gets a real automatic knowledge of how to suck it. Doesn't he? Greg, you keep that up for much longer and I am going to be shooting my whole load at you, so unless you think you are up for taking a mouth full of man cum juice in your gut, you had better be ready to pull off of that dick when I let out a scream that I'm getting real ready! And Greg, — the way you are using my dick right now, the way you are going at it, it is going to be pretty damn soon, man,—ugh Greg, get ready man! Greg I'm getting real close to cumin man! Greg, I'm telling you man—I'm getting real close! Greg—Greg—unless you want a mouthful, you better get off of my dick!"

Greg made no attempt to pull off of Sam. He grabbed Sam even that much tighter and pulled Sam into his face as strongly as he could. He was acting like a cock sucker that had been doing this for a long time! Sam was shocked at Greg's strength at pulling him up as tightly to his face as he was doing! Suddenly Sam knew that Greg was very well aware that he was just about to get a mouth full of man cum, and Sam knew that Greg was wanting it, and he was wanting it now, and he was wanting it forcefully!

"Greg! I'mmmmm —cuminnnnnnnn man!! Oh shit Greg! Greg, I shot all my load in you! You OK? I sure as the hell never expected you to take my load man! Shit Greg, most guys just don't do that on their first dick. God man! That shocked the hell out of me that you grabbed me and pulled me into your mouth like that! Greg, you completely locked us together. Shit man, there was no way of pulling out of your mouth! Shit man, you clamped onto me totally! God

Greg! Man, I don't know if I've ever been with another guy that took all my cum the very first time he sucked on a dick! Shit man! What a shock! You OK?"

"Yeah I'm OK." Greg managed to get out as he continued to swallow Sam's cum that was still in his mouth! "Yeah, Oh shit Sam, I did not expect to do that. Hell I was so damn afraid to even put your dick in my mouth when we started, and now I've got so damn much of your cum down in my gut that if guys could have kids, I'd be carrying around one of yours. Oh shit man! It feels like you dumped a gallon of juice in me. Oh Sam, no way in hell did I ever think that I would get so damn excited that I wouldn't be able to pull off of you when I knew you were getting ready! Oh man! Hey—what a fucking trip man, what a fucking trip! Sam—you have just turned me into what I guess I would call a true cock sucker! Sam, while I was sucking on you, I just couldn't forget what you told me about me getting my ass fucked by that damn big rod in there! I just kept getting hotter and hotter just thinking about that happening! Sam, I've got to get fucked by Jack! Is it OK if I let him be the first guy up in my butt? Sam, I just have to know that his dick was the first dick I've ever taken up in me! Sam, I'm really getting all funny over this stuff. I've dreamt about getting to do something like this for years now, and I'm finally getting to do it, and I almost feel like I can't stop! Oh Sam, I want to suck on you and get fucked by Jack all at the same time! Oh Sam I want you in my mouth and him in my ass all at the same time! Oh Sam I want to know whenever I see Jack around the apartment complex, that I've had his dick up in my ass. Oh Sam, just imagine me and Susan talking to Jack sometime, and while she's standing there with me, me knowing that I got fucked by that guy! Oh shit man! Can you imagine us standing there and I can't tell her that Jack, that great big muscle guy, has fucked my ass with his great big black rod! Oh man,—just the idea of standing there and being right in front of that great big crotch and not being able to tell Susan that he's got one fucking big enormous cock hidden in those pants, and he's fucked my ass with it the same way I fuck her! Oh man, just knowing he'll be standing there, fully knowing what it feels like to fuck my little white ass with that big cock, pushing that damn thing up in me as far as it will go, and not be able to say anything about it!"

"Sam, every time I see that man, maybe him just walking through the complex, or maybe him in the office, or even maybe him at a restaurant, I wanna know inside of me, that I had his big black dick up inside of me, and I can't tell anybody that I did! I want him to be able to look at me and him remembering that he had his big rod stuck up in my ass. I want him to know he was the very first guy to spread my ass and push his dick up in there! I want him to take me for my very first time! I wanna remember this day forever! I do! I wanna be able to just close my eyes and just feel him going back up in me, all over again!"

"Oh Sam, —I've never been this fucking horny before! Oh God Sam, please tell Jack I really do want to get it up in the ass with his dick! Oh shit man, I hope like hell I don't regret this! It's going to hurt like hell, isn't it? I know it's got to hurt to put something that damn big up in your ass! Doesn't it? It's got to, doesn't it? Oh shit Sam, I'm so fucking hot and horny! I know it's got to hurt, but Sam, I really do want to know I got fucked by him! I've dreamt of something like this happening to me for way too long! Oh Sam, how many nights have I gone to sleep dreaming about something like this actually happening. Oh Sam, I never thought I'd ever get to do it! Of all of the times that I have dreamt about something like this happening to me, never, did I ever think that maybe it could be with some guy that is as big and as strong and muscled and hung as big and as long as Jack is! I want to know Jack has fucked me! Every time I see him I want to know he's used me and he's used my ass! I want to know he was the first guy to fuck my ass! I want to know he's had all of it up inside of me! I know it's going to hurt when he does it, but I guess I'll suffer that just to know he's fucked me. Once it's done, then I'll always be able to know he did me at least once! I want to be able to just watch him while he works and just know his great big black dick was the first dick I ever took up in my ass! Sam, let's go in there with them so Jack can fuck my ass. I want to suck on you while he is fucking me! OK? You'll help me get fucked by him, won't you?

You'll hold me while he fucks me won't you? Oh Sam, I can't believe this! Oh man, I'm finally going to get my ass fucked! Oh yeah Sam, I need this! Oh God, I've wanted this for years! I want to know I got fucked! And Sam, I know now I want to get fucked big time! Oh yeah, I want that big dick up in me! I want it in my ass! I want every story I've ever read about some guy getting fucked in the ass, to become me today! I really do want to be that guy, the one that really gets fucked and fucked hard! Every time I ever see some gay porn showing some guy getting it in the ass, I wanna just say, "Yeah, but I got it bigger and better than you did! "

CHAPTER SEVEN:

A First Time for Everything

Sam and Greg went into the master bedroom and found Jim, yes—Jim, fucking the hell out of Jack's ass.

"Shit man!" Sam expounded. "Hell man, I thought for sure we'd find Jim getting all of your big rod up in his ass, Jack, —not you, —getting his up in you! This is kind of a surprising turn around!"

Jack turned, looked at Sam and Greg and replied, "Yeah, I know! I'm usually the guy on top and in some other guy's ass, but Jim convinced me that I needed to feel a dick up my ass once in awhile, so anyway, he's pounding me for a change. Hey guys, how did it go in the other room?"

"Well, pretty damn well, I'd say!" Replied Sam.

"Greg has now had his cock sucked, he liked that, and he has now sucked cock, and he likes that too!"

"What? He sucked you? Hey, Greg, congratulations man, congrads!" Jack actively said, and was followed with Jim's, "Hey great going man!"

"Yeah he sucked and got sucked and now he is wanting to get fucked in the ole butt hole! And guess just who he wants to be the first guy up in there?!"

Jim looked over at Sam as he continued to pump Jack's ass and asked, "Well, I thought you guys were going to go in there and let him get your dick Sam. I thought that was what you two were planning on doing, was getting him fucked a little so he knew he could take it OK."

"Well yeah-that was kind of the plan, but you know how things can change. We did some good serious sucking, and Greg now knows that doing this stuff is OK, and he has decided that if it was OK with everybody he'd like to just always be able to remember that Jack was the first dick up in his ass. He knows that the idea of getting one that big up in there the very first time he gets fucked is exciting, and something that can never be changed, so I told him, that we'd come in here and let Jack know he has a very virgin ass needing some attention."

Jack watched and listened as Sam explained just what had happened, and what was going to happen, and he grinned very widely, and said, "Yeah man! Yeah! Greg, I will be more than happy to be the first dick up in that coach's ass. You, just having the idea of knowing that it was my dick up in there first is exciting, but let me tell you man, the idea that I get to be the first one to evade that little hole is exciting to me. Let our friend Jim get his rocks off in my butt here, and I will be more than glad to accommodate your hungry desires!"

As Jim continued to fuck Jack's strong muscular mahogany butt, Sam and Greg spread out on the other side of the bed, and managed to keep each others dicks rock hard with some nice gentle rubbing and massaging.

Sam looked at Jack and asked, "Has he been fucking you ever since you two came in here?"

"No, no!" Jack replied. "No! Jim had to see if he could hold my dick down into his throat as far as it would go for five minutes without pulling off of it to get some breath. He did pretty well. He choked a couple of times, but he managed to stay on it, and I think maybe he hit his goal. He tried to pull off two or three times, but with my hands locked around his head, he found out pretty quickly that he needed to breath through his nose and not try to breathe through his mouth. His mouth was pretty full, and I wasn't going to be the one blamed for him not getting his goal of five minutes. Didn't you guys hear him coughing and choking when he finally got me out of him? He sat here for another five minutes and tried to regain his breath!"

Without a word, Jack, Sam and Greg knew that Jim was in the process of doing one hot male climaxing and was loading Jack's ass with his little white man cum. Jack could feel Jim's body tighten up, go rigid, Jim's rod being pushed down into his ass even farther than it had been, and Sam and Greg could tell from the expression on Jim's face that his dick was now in the process of doing its manly thing, and that was letting the man juices fly!

Unconsciously Sam and Greg both encouraged by uttering, "Yeah, go man go!"

After Jim re-gained some composure, pulled his now exhausted cock from the confines of Jack's strong, tight, muscular ass, and wiped the sweat from his forehead, he then looked at Greg and asked, "Get fucked by Jack? Are you real sure you want to do that?"

Before Greg had any chance to answer, Sam jumped in, "Yeah Jim, he does! We talked about it and he wants to always know that it was Jack's big rod that he took first. He knows he's in for a challenge, but I think right now that just might be part of it. He asked me if I'd help him get fucked by Jack. We know it might take some time, but once Greg got used to doing some sucking and getting sucked, he's realized that he has finally gotten himself involved in some activity that he has been wanting for a long time, so I think he's man enough to do it!"

Then looking at Jack, Sam continued, "Jack, he wants you and he knows it's going to hurt when you push it in, but he told me that he will suffer that just to know you fucked him first. That rod of yours and its size has really gotten him all turned on, so are you willing to take it good and slow until he gets you up in there?"

"Hey no problem," Jack reassured. "Hey Greg your ass is not the first ass that got started by using my dick up in it. A few of years ago when I was working at an office building on the night cleaning crew, one of the guys there found a gay magazine hidden in a cabinet in the men's room, and when he found it, he showed it to me and then started talking about some of the pictures in it. It became very obvious that he was a little more interested in the actions showing in the pictures, than the actual magazine. I often wondered if maybe he had placed that magazine there himself just so he could bring up the subject of gay sex. He was cute, damn well build, aged about 22 or 23, and found out later, pretty damn well hung."

"Uhhhh, —pretty damn well hung? Just how did you find that out Jack?" Sam quickly asked.

"Hey guy, when you are always anxious for some good tight male ass, and you got a guy like that Georgie guy around you asking for help on understanding things like gay sex, a man's gotta do, what a man's gotta do! Right?"

Looking at Jack, Greg then asked, "Do as in do? Do what?"

"Do the ass! Hey after just so much talking and hinting, and some more hinting, I finally decided that what this guy really needed was a hands on learning experience! And I decided I was gonna be the teacher. Hey guys, it was a black ass, and I had never fucked a black ass! Every ass I have ever fucked around with was a white ass, and so I decided, why not!"

One night during supper break, I was in the supply room with only Georgie, and as I grabbed my basket and kind of jerked it back and forth some, and I asked him, 'Hey Georgie. I'm not gonna be busy after we get done here tonight. Wanna come over to my place and have a beer, or something?' It was when I asked the, 'or something,' that I really jerked my dick around some. He obviously saw it, and I guess he understood what I meant, cause he immediately told me yes, yeah he wanted to come over for a beer, and he grinned when he said, 'a beer.' He knew damn well what I was thinking!"

"We got done working, headed over to my house, got a couple of beers, and I took off my clothes! He just sat there and looked. I looked at him and asked if he was gonna get naked or not! That was the first time that I learned that he had never been with a guy before. He admitted that ever since he had been working there, he had been wanting to do some good and nasty stuff with me, but he didn't know how to let me know. He finally admitted that the magazine thing was his way of trying to get to start talking gay stuff with me. He admitted that at first he didn't know if I was gay, or would even do anything with a guy like that or not, but then he decided that I knew so much about what guys do together, that it was safe to make a stab at it, to see if he could get together. He told me that he wanted to do some stuff, but he didn't know how. I told him that the first thing he needed to learn is how to get fucked in the ass!"

"Jack, you taught him how, I assume, right?" Sammy asked.

"Yeah, yeah I sure did! He was one anxious guy. There sure wasn't too much learning or teaching going on that night, though! That ass was hot and ready! I really don't think Georgie really knew it himself, but I think he was wanting to get it in the ass, all along, and just did not know it, or didn't know how to say what he wanted."

"Jack did he take all of your dick right away?" Jim anxiously asked as he once again checked out the pillar of meat that Jack was supporting.

"Oh yeah! Yeah he did! He let out one little yell when I really punched it all the way in, but you know guys, when a hole is really ready and really hungry, the man under that hole is begging to get it all filled up fast. That was Georgie that night. He wanted it and he had finally found the way to get it. And what an ass it was! God man, what a hard, firm tight ass that was! I already said I thought I was more anxious about fucking him than he was about getting fucked, and let me tell you guys, once I was in there and pushing with all of my might, I sure as hell was glad he had the guts to tell me he wanted me to do stuff with me, even though he didn't know just what! Shit was he good!"

"Yeah, and soon I kinda guess he liked my ass too. We were doing each other then."

"Doing each other!? Did he fuck you?"

"Sure, yeah! He asked me one night if he could do that since he had never fucked some guy,—he had just gotten fucked, and I told him sure! Why not? I like a dick up my ass like everybody else does, I guess."

"So how long did you two do it? Did you guys do it for quite awhile?" Jim asked with some jealousy sounding in his voice.

"Oh Georgie and I fucked each other for about two years or a little more. We kinda played with another one of the crew one night, but that didn't work out so well!"

"When Butch found out that Georgie and I were playing with each other, he decided he wanted to be part of it. Well, that was until I took my pants off and my 11 inches sprung out. Butch's ass got all up-tight and scared. I never did get to fuck him. He watched me fuck the hell out of Georgie's ass, but he just never got the nerve to let me put it up in him. He just kept telling us how he had never even seen one that fucking big before, and hell no, it was not going up in his ass. So I never got to fuck Butch's hole. He sure as hell had a greater appreciation for what Georgie could take though! He kept telling Georgie, "Oh shit man, I can not believe it! I can not believe you can take that much up in your ass like that! Damn I can not believe it!"

"Oh come on man, I've got to take it now man! Oh shit man you have got me so fucking turned on telling me that, —come on, —let me find out if I can take it or not! Come on please Jack, please show me I can take it! Please, please fuck me!" Greg pleaded and begged.

"Ok man, I'm ready. Sorry, —kind of guess we all kind of got carried away with my little story about doing Georgie and fucking his ass for its first time, didn't we? Hey Greg, lay down there on your stomach and let me at that hot ass of yours. OK? It's not a hot black ass like Georgie's was, but let me tell you it is one hell of a hot white ass. This ass is gonna look fucking good in the school, with your tight coach's shorts hugging it, kissing it, and all the boy and girls looking at it as you stroll down the hallways! Gonna be a lot of lips licked as you stroll along just acting like the good ole straight coach! Hell man, just you wait till the daddies start coming to the school just to talk about their kids on the teams. Hell man, they ain't gonna be concerned if little Jimmy or little Janie are on the team or not, they're just gonna wanna make sure you and that hot ass and hot bod of yours is on their team, or maybe on your team! You're gonna be one fucking hot coach man, fucking hot!"

As Greg laid down, he said "Thanks" but also started having more second thoughts and said, "Oh fuck man, oh shit! Oh, God, now that I've begged for it, oh shit, now I'm getting scared. Oh crap man! Oh shit, should I be doing this?"

"Hey tell you what. Jim why don't you get up there by Greg's head so he can maybe grab ahold of you or maybe stick your dick in his mouth and you can rub his head or shoulders and assure him everything back here is going to be OK! OK?" Jack suggested.

"Sammy what you going to do while I break in this virgin ass?"

"Right now I'm just going to sit here and watch that damn big thing slide up into Greg's ass and kind of give him a minute to minute up-date of how it's going on this end, then after it's up and in him and he knows he's still got an ass, I think maybe I will slam my face up in that hot, tight, mahogany butt of yours and let you slam my face with it while you poke his ass."

"Oh shit man! That sounds great! I need a good tongue licking back there anyway. Hey Greg, I'm going to push some KY jelly up in your butt, so don't jump when you feel my fingers going up in there, OK?"

"Ok yeah! Oh shit man, am I crazy for doing this? Oh God man maybe that Butch guy was right. Maybe I should be yelling, 'No way in hell!' Oh man! Hey Jim, let me grab hold of you. Oh,- I've never had anybody put stuff up in my ass before, and now I think I'm going to be able to take that fucking pole? I'm crazy man, I fucking crazy! I've got to be!"

"No you're not Greg!" Jim quickly reassured him. "Jack told you other guys have taken his dick for their first fucking, and I know damn well you can too. Remember earlier how set you were in making sure Jack's rod was the first one you took? Lay there and relax. Here, lay your head in my lap and grab hold of my waist. Yeah-there! Better?"

"Oh God man I guess but I'm getting real scared now that my ass is going to hurt like hell when he puts that up in me! Oh man, I swear I'm fucking crazy for doing this! I swear I must be!"

"No, you're not! You're OK!" Sammy reassured him. "Greg you're OK and in about a minute or two you will be so glad you did this you'll wish you had been doing this for years. There, feel Jack's fingers putting that KY up in you? Hey Jack, rub the inside of his ass for a minute to get it all excited about getting something up in there. Yeah—there feel that Greg? Like that?"

"Oh yeah I can feel that! Yeah that feels kind of good, but really feels a lot different than anything I've felt back there before. Hey, Sam, how many fingers he got up in me? Has he got his whole hand up in there?"

"No, no, —not hardly Greg! Not hardly! Right now he's only got two fingers in you. Feel like a lot more?"

"Oh hell yes! Oh God man if he's only got two fingers up in me right now, —oh shit man what in the hell is it going to feel like when he puts that fucking big dick of his up in me? Oh man! Oh shit man, —can I really do this?"

"Hey cool down man, cool down!" Sam again reassured Greg. "Seriously Greg your ass will open up a hell of a lot quicker than what you might think. Just lay there and grab ahold of Jim. Hey, put your face in his lap and maybe lick on his dick for a minute. Jack's not going to hurt you any. Besides, remember how excited you were to get it? Well, hang in there man, pretty soon you'll be able to say you took it!"

"Hey Greg, I'm going to kind of get my dick all aimed up here, but don't panic, —I will go real slow! I'm serious man, I'll go slow so this feels good, OK?"

"Yeah OK! Yeah I guess. Oh shit man, I've got to be one fucking crazy guy to let you do me! Oh Jim, hang onto me!"

"Hey Greg, lay still and hang onto Jim. Jacks got you all greased up and has kind of gotten your ass opened some with his fingers, so just lay there and let him do this and enjoy it! OK?' Sammy asked.

"Oh God yeah I guess it's OK. I was the one that said I wanted it, but shit man, now I'm wondering! Oh God! Oh shit! He's starting in, isn't he Sam? Oh shit man, he's starting to put that up in me isn't he? Oh God man can I take it? Oh shit man I'm scared! He said it's eleven inches long didn't he? Oh God man! If it goes all the way in, will I be able to walk, later? Oh crap man, oh shit! It's going up in my ass isn't it?"

"Just a little, Greg, just a little. Lay there and let your ass relax. Yeah, relax it man, relax it!" Sam suggested and encouraged.

"Oh shit man, that's easy for you to say! Sam it's not your ass that's about ready to get a steam roller slammed up in it. Oh God he's pushing more up in me isn't he? Oh I can feel him pushing it up in me! Oh, I can feel it moving! Oh I can feel it up in me!"

"Yeah Greg, yeah he is, but he's going slow. He's taking your ass real slow. Don't get to anxious thinking more is going on back here than what is! He's going in real slow!"

"Ouch, —oh shit, —oh shit, —oh shit! Oh man that stung! Oh God man that stung for a second there! Oh Sam was that supposed to hurt like that?"

"Yeah Greg, when he opened up the tight little ring up inside it does for a second, but he's got it open now. He's got his dick in that ring now! That was just kind of like pushing open a tight rubber band. He's got it stretched open now! Now it's kinda like he's got his dick stuck up in the wedding ring! See, that makes it feel better now, doesn't it? Now man, it's all good and fun from here on out, or maybe I should say from here on in! Lay still, all Jack needs to do now is lay there on your butt and just push it on in. Greg, this is going to feel great! In just a minute you are going to feel that rod all the way up in you, and you are going to be so fucking glad you did this! Grab Jimmy there and love on his crotch while Jack makes you a real man!"

"Oh Greg your ass feels good, so good!" Jack stated as he continued to fill Greg's virgin hole. "Lay still man, I'm making progress back here and in just a minute, you and I are going to be one man. All of my dick is going to be up inside of you and we're going to be feeling like we are just one guy stuck together! You OK? You feeling this up in you? You like it?"

"Oh yeah man—oh yeah I can feel it! God 'O mighty it feels big! Shit man, how much you got in me now?"

"He's got just about half of it in right now Greg. Lay still and let him feed you the rest! You've already got your ass open and taking it, —now it's just let him feed in the rest of it. Ok? You ok?"

"Half of it!? He's only got half of it in me so far? Oh God can I take the rest? Oh shit man, I feel full already!"

"Hey relax man, relax! Jack's going real slow and easy and you are doing just fine! Seriously Greg, once he gets the whole thing up in there, that's when your ass is going to start jumping and you are going to be begging for him feed you more and to pound it as hard as he can." Sam again reassured Greg.

"Hey Sam!" Jack said. "Why don't you get yourself up there by Jim and kind of stand over him and Greg and let me suck on your dick while I do Greg here. You can stand there and let me have your dick in my mouth and let your man lick on your butt for a little while. OK?"

"Oh hell yes!" Sammy immediately responded. With Sam in the new position everybody was involved in the action. Greg was face down on the bed, and of course with Jack and his railroad car dick sliding up into the depths of his ass, his face was laying on Jim's crotch, with his tongue every once in awhile licking on Jim's meat, —when he wasn't expressing his concerns about if he could really take the rest of Jack's rod, and of course Sam was positioned so that he could fuck Jack's mouth and at the same time get his ass licked and sucked on by his lover, Jim. Everybody was enjoying the multiple person activity and rather keeping Greg's mind off of the action still going on in his ass.

"Oh man! Oh yeah!" All of a sudden Jack let out. "Oh man, I'm in! I'm in all the way Greg! You have me! You've got all of it! It's all up in you man! How you feeling? You OK? How you doing man?"

"Oh Jack push on my butt! Oh yeah,-oh yeah! Oh man that is good! You really have all of that big thing up in me? You sure? Oh I can't believe you have all of that up in me! Jack you sure it's all the way in?"

"Yeah man, yeah! I'm pushing on your tight ass as hard as I can and it is all up in there! See, that wasn't so bad now was it? See how easy it is to take it?"

"Oh Jack I can't believe you have all of it up in me! Oh man, that does feel food! Yeah, man, it does feel good! Oh shit I thought it was going to hurt when you put it all the way up in me. I was afraid that it was gonna feel like I was having a kid when you got it all the way up in there! Man, that's better than when you first started. Oh Jack, yeah, pump me man, pump me! Oh yeah man! Oh yes! Yeah, you guys were right! It does feel good! Oh how in the hell can that much dick, stuck up in your ass, feel so good? Oh my God, I'm glad I had you fuck me! Oh yeah this is good! Yeah, I like this! Oh shit man, this is great! Yeah Jack, now fuck the hell out of me! Yeah man, yeah! That is good! Oh my God man, don't ever get out of my ass!"

Hearing that excitement Sammy immediately changed positions and said, "Jack I've got to suck on your ass while you fuck him! I've got to put my face up in there and feel you fucking him from back there!"

Sam positioned himself so that his face was tucked in, right up by the crack and hole —between the solid black ass muscles that Jack was flexing, as he pumped the "new man's" ass.

Sam was ass sucking, Jack was ass fucking, Jim was getting sucked on and Greg, well he was in total heaven getting it up the ass about half way to his throat and at the same time getting Jim's dick stuck down his throat from the other direction.

All four men took advantage of the activity for at least 15 or 20 minutes when all of a sudden, Jack yelled, "Oh man, oh man, I'm going to cum! I'm gonna do it guys, I'm about ready to cum!"

Jack immediately pulled his entire length out of Greg's ass and without time to say anything else, he let fly!

Looking around Jack's torso, Sammy watched the juices fly and he exclaimed, "Oh my God Jack! Oh shit man, —look at what you just let loose! Oh shit man, —haven't you shot off for a week or something?"

As Greg was laying there, all of a sudden he felt the warm juices hit his back. "Oh man! Oh man is that all cum? Man that is warm! Jack did you pee on me or is that all cum I feel on my back?"

"Hey young tight ass, —that is all cum! You and your tight ass made me shoot like I have not shot for a long time! Man, that ass of yours is good! Oh Greg, thank you for letting me be the first guy up in there! Wow man! What a fuck! Shit, — I'm exhausted! Greg man, you do know now that every time I see you around the apartment complex that I'm gonna get a ragging hard on just remembering that I was the first guy to get up in there! There's always a first time for everything, and man, that was the first time for that! There will never be another guy that will ever be able to say that he fucked you first! Damn man, that was great, great!"

CHAPTER EIGHT:

I knew I Had a Chance!

Jack went into his maintenance office and immediately checked his messages, to see if there were any emergency repairs that needed to be done. One, —one that had just been called in about five minutes earlier from apartment 187. It was now, 7:30 AM, on this Saturday morning, so whoever had the problem, Jack decided, they apparently must have found it when they got up that morning. Jack's normal Saturday mornings were just normally doing some "catch-up" items that maybe needed to be finished, but of course any emergency items always got top priority.

After grabbing his address book of apartment residences and repair notes, Jack read: "Apartment 187 — Barbara and Stan Hughes, two residents, no pet, move in date, September 3, 2004." There were no repair notes, so obviously no prior work had been required at that apartment since they had moved in, and as Jack stood there, he tried to remember if he had ever met this particular couple. As he read the line "Occupation" and the entry did say, "Bank Security Guard", he immediately did remember seeing Stan around the complex! The hot built muscle guy that wore his security uniform like it was special made for him! Jack kind of looked up toward the ceiling, and thought, maybe not a real tall guy, —maybe five foot nine or ten, —but what he didn't have in height, he sure as hell did make up for it, in bulk, solid bulk! Suddenly Jack had a much higher anxiety for taking care of this apartment call than he originally had, and especially, —since the voice on the message was a man's voice, and not a lady's.

Jack dialed the apartment phone number and had a very short conversation with Stan, whose identity had been confirmed, and Jack asked if this was going to be a convenient time for him to come by, to make the repair. Stan assured him that it certainly would be, and in fact, since the toilet would not stop running on its own, fixing it as soon as possible would be appreciated.

When Jack knocked on the door at apartment 187, the door immediately came open, and Stan then opened the screen door, to let Jack come in.

"Good morning, I'm Jack Jensen."

Extending his hand out for a handshake, Stan replied, "Good morning, I'm Stan Hughes. Thanks for coming so soon. Didn't know if you'd be available today or not. Come on in, the bathroom's right down here, and the problem is a toilet that just doesn't want to stop running on its own. Just started doing that, we didn't have any problems earlier."

As Jack shook Stan's hand, and admired the strength that Stan transposed through that hand, he tried to listen to what Stan was saying, but internally he had to admit that the sight he was confronted with was making it very hard to concentrate on words. "My God man, does he know what he's showing?" Jack kept thinking over and over as he tried to so slightly look up and down the body of muscles that was standing there in front of him, —with only a pair of tight, very tight, white thigh length Calvin Klein boxer brief, under shorts on, and a dick of glory, laying sideways to the left.

Not fully stiff, but certainly not laying there as if in complete relaxed mode. If it wasn't in the process of getting excited, then it had to be in the "come back down" mode! Jack knew he wanted to just reach out and feel it! He wanted to rub his hand on it and feel it get bigger and stronger! He knew it was not at its full extension, and he was anxious to help it get to that point. Stan made no mention of having almost nothing on, nor any mention of his manly physical part that was either half way up, or half way down, and he acted as if this was his normal attire.

As Stan turned to walk down the hall, Jack took advantage of being behind Stan, and he took in every bit of looking and admiring that he could, for the less than one half minute that it took to go to the bathroom. "My God man! What a tight ass that guy has got! Shit man, look at those legs! I can't imagine some guy looking like that, and especially since he knew I was coming over right away! Wait! Wait-he knew I was gonna be coming over. He could have put on some shorts or something if he'd wanted to!"

Jack went into the bathroom and as he removed the top of the toilet tank, he knew that Stan had gone into the bedroom and was not standing beside him any longer. With a lot of wonderment in his mind about just why Stan had not put more clothes on before he came into the apartment, he decided that "maybe, just maybe" he needed to go to his maintenance shop to get "something," anything, just so he'd have a reason to maybe walk past and check out the bedroom, to see just what Stan was doing at that time. "Hell man, he might be just getting dressed, and I'm getting myself all excited about nothing. Maybe the man just doesn't get all nervous and embarrassed to have another guy see him."

Following through with his little scheme of needing to go back for "something" at the maintenance shop, Jack hollered out to Stan, "Hey Stan, I need to go to the maintenance room and get some washers, I'll be right back. OK?"

Stan stepped out into the hall and returned the comment with an, "OK. Don't bother knocking at the door when you come back. It's just you and me here anyway, so just come on back in. Barbara's at work, so don't worry bout walking in on her, OK?"

Jack once again looked at Stan, and all of his exposed muscles, and answered an, "OK. I'll be right back!"

"He's sure not getting dressed, I can see that!" Jack pondered as he then turned and headed for the door. "That damn dick of his is getting me so fucking turned on, me wanting it in my mouth, —that I'm having some real problems keeping my mind on the job."

Just as Jack got back to his maintenance shop, he grabbed the phone and dialed Jim and Sammy's apartment 117. Jim answered the phone. "Jim, God Jim, you will not believe what in the hell is going on. Jim I am so fucking flustered I can't hardly handle myself!"

"Jack, what in the hell are you talking about man, what is going on?"

Jack quickly told Jim about Stan and how Stan was hardly dressed, showing his muscles and his big dick, and was very definite when he pointed out that Barbara was at work, and how he was instructed to just come back in when he went back to the apartment.

"Jack, right now all I can tell you is, —go for it! If it's that bank security guy that I've seen coming and going in the parking lot, go for it! If he even slightly suggests something, go for it! I think he's trying to tell you something, and I think his firm statement about Barbara being at work, is a total statement of wanting you to make a move! Seriously man, I think he's asking for it. Was his toilet really having a problem?"

"No Jim, no! That was another thing I wondered about. All he needed to do was bend one little metal piece just a little, and in fact, I wonder if maybe he bent it earlier, just so he could call for me to come over! Oh Jim, I think he wants it, and if so, I'm gonna do him. Thanks man, thanks, I'll let you know what happens! Bye, gotta go!"

"Bye Jack, and don't forget, if you need to or wanna get him again in the future, you can always use our place. Fact is, tell him to come over here anytime! Sam and I'll take care of him. Bye, let me know what happens!"

Jack grabbed a few washers so that he'd at least look like he needed them when he got back to the apartment, and he headed back for apartment 187. Remembering what Stan had said about not knocking, he opened the door, stepped in, and realized that he heard the shower running. Stopping for a moment in the hallway, Jack then went on into the bathroom and much to his shock, amassment, but yet shear complete joy, he was confronted with the view of Stan, standing in the clear glass shower, showering and at the same time, —jerking himself off!

Looking out at Jack, now numbly standing there with his mouth hanging open, Stan yelled out, "Come on in, I wanna scrub you down!"

Shocked beyond belief, Jack continued to stand there as he attempted to regain control of his mind. The totally unexpected sight of Stan being fully naked, and now also in the hot process of jerking himself off, right there in front of him, was shocking, but yet totally exciting to Jack. He felt his heart step up about three beats and he also felt his dick getting bigger and bigger!

"Come on man, come on!" Stan again yelled out! "Hey guy, I've wanted you and me to shower together ever since I saw you last month working on the sign out front. Come on, I know you want to too, don't you? Come on man, I'm about to let this thing fly and I want it on you! Come on, nobody's gonna know! Just you and me! Come on. Let me squirt on you! It'll turn me on like you can't believe! Come on man, I wanna feel you and that damn big dick I'm sure you're hanging in there!"

Stan's words, and his excited actions on his dick were definitely making Jack hornier than he had been in weeks. As he licked his lips, rubbed his crotch, and took a very deep breath, he immediately started stripping everything off and getting himself ready to join Stan in the shower.

"Oh yeah man, yeah!" Stan exclaimed as he watched Jack strip everything off! "Oh shit man, God you've got the dick of death on you man, what a fucking rod! Oh come on man, let me at it, let me at it!"

Stan's excitement had completely overtaken Jack and his hesitation about if this was really the right thing to do or not! He knew he had lost all control over right or wrong. This man was horny, hot, built, and begging for him to get in the shower with him, and he was gonna do it! Jack thought, "Oh shit man. Even if I had never played with some guy before, I think this is what could have gotten me into it! This fucker is hot, and I'm gonna get me some of him. He wants me, and damn man, I'm going for it. On the job or not, straight, or gay, this is way too much for any sucker to turn down!"

As Jack approached the shower door, Stan opened it up and smiled as Jack stepped in. "Oh yeah man, oh yeah! Oh man, what a fucking body you got on you! God man, your dick is like two root beer cans glued end to end and sticking out in front of you! God man, that is one fucking big rod! Pretty as hell, but one hell of a lot bigger than any dicks I've ever seen! Oh God man, I knew the first time I saw you I needed you! Jack, you are one fucking god! Oh shit man, when I saw you walking in from the parking lot this morning, I knew today had to be the day I finally got you! Oh shit man, you are fucking hot! I watched that crotch of yours each and every step you took. I could just imagine that dick tucked in there and those baseballs rubbing up against your legs! Damn man, I wish I had a dick and two balls like that! How in the hell do you ever put pants on and not show everything that's tucked inside! Damn man, I love it, I do! I wish I had stuff tucked inside like that, I do! Man I'd love to see what that basket looks like in a pair of Speedos! Shit man, that basket has got to stand out like it's got a fucking cantaloupe stuffed in there! If you put Speedos on, I'll bet people think you've stuffed a big fucking squash up in there don't they?"

As Stan told Jack how hot he was for getting to play with Jack, he continued, but yet even faster, continued to jerk on his own hunk of meat, and at the same time lean over toward Jack and take his left tit into his mouth and suck on it!

"Yeah man, yeah! Suck on it man, suck on it!" Jack encouraged as Stan continued to jerk his meat and slightly nibble on Jack's tit!

"Oh yes man, oh yes! Yeah, that feels good! Bite it man, bite it! Yeah man, yeah!"

Stan sucked and bit on Jack's tits, back and forth, left to right and back again, and then slid his tongue right down the middle of Jack's chest, down along the full length of his dick, and then down and under it!

"Yeah, get your mouth down there and suck a nut dry man, suck a nut dry! Suck 'em in your mouth and make me feel 'em getting jerked around in there man, make me feel it! Suck a black nut man, suck a black nut! "

Stan's left hand was engaged in his jerking off, and his right hand was now in the process of finding Jack's crack, back on the back side, right in between the two hard slabs of firm, tight, black, ass cheeks. He was now finger fucking the stud that he had seen up on the ladder fixing the sign, and now he was right where he had wished he was at that day! His face right up in the hunk's crotch, and his fingers in his hole!

Jack was now fully in the process of presenting himself completely to Stan, for whatever actions Stan desired and wanted. He had his mouth on his nuts, and his fingers up in his ass, so he really did not think there was much that he could say was off base! He had fully overcome his earlier questions about if he should be doing this or not. Stan had successfully accomplished getting Jack, not only into the mood, but also fully into the actions.

Stan continued to jerk on his rod, as he now switched back up to Jack's chest and from Jack's left tit, over to his right tit. Jack threw his chest forward, encouraging all of the sucking and biting, and nibbling, that Stan was doing on both of the tits. As he encouraged Stan's actions, —actions that were getting Jack more and more excited, Jack grabbed ahold of his own dick and started his own jerking action. He did not need to work it into a hard state of being, it had already accomplished that as he stepped into the shower.

Suddenly Stan pulled off of Jack's tits and knelt down on his knees in front of the 11 inch rod that was now directly in front of his face. "Oh my God man, can I take this? Oh Jack, can I take this? Do guys get all of this down their throats? Oh shit man, oh man, I gotta see what I can do!"

And with that statement and exclamation of desire, want and excitement, Stan opened his mouth as widely as possible and actually threw his head onto Jack's ragging hard on! Jack grabbed the back of his head and pulled him forward as much as possible! Inch by inch, his thick stiff rod disappeared down into Stan's mouth. Struggling and forcing it with every bit of excitement he had, Stan managed to open up his throat wider than he had ever been forced to do before! This was the biggest hunk of meat that he had ever attempted to get in his mouth, —dick or streak!

"Suck me man, suck me! Suck me! Suck me!! Suck me!!!" Jack actually yelled as Stan managed to get more and more of the big dark mahogany rod down into his throat! "Yeah, yeah, yeah! Yeah, make me feel you suck on me man! Suck on me! Oh Stan, do me man, do me!"

As Jack was yelling for Stan to suck on him, and to suck on him hard, he realized that as he was now looking down, watching Stan work on his dick. Stan was in the process of letting all of his jazz juices go flying. That sight turned Jack on even that much higher and he once again grabbed Stan by the back of his head and actually locked himself inside of Stan's mouth.

Suddenly realizing that Stan was now pushing against him, and rather slapping his legs, Jack realized that he was suffocating Stan by holding him so tightly up against himself, and he let loose of Stan's head.

"Wow, oh shit!" Stan uttered as he attempted to regain some oxygen. "Shit man, you've got too much dick to let a man breathe. Wow, what a fucking throat full!" Then looking up at Jack, he asked, "Jack, have you ever been sucked on before? Have you ever let other guys at this thing?"

Looking down at Stan, still on his knees and right in front of the dick of conversation, Jack replied, "Oh yeah man! Oh yeah! Down their throats and up their tight little asses! Yeah, you sure ain't the first guy on that dick! Hell man, it's been sucked on so much, I'm surprised they ain't sucked the color out of it already! From the way you took it, I sure do know that ain't the first dick you've ever sucked on before is it?"

"Not the first dick, but sure as hell the first dick that size! My god man, that thing is enormous. Seriously man, that is like trying to suck on the end of a fire hose! And when it shoots cum shots, I'll bet they'd feel like fire hose water too! Love it, love it! After that one, I'm afraid some small one's not gonna make it for me anymore! Beautiful, beautiful!"

"Beautiful and still full! You shot your load, I saw it flying to the floor, that's what made me grab you so damn tight, but my dick's still got about a quart of cum up in there! You want it? Ready to take it man, ready? Every eaten some hot cum for a big long black dick before?"

"I've eaten some cum before, but no, —never out of a big black dick. Jack, that was one of the reasons I made a pact with myself that day I saw you up on that ladder working on that sign out front. I walked past you, looked up at you, saw that crotch sticking out of the front of you, and that day, I told myself I was gonna get you, I wanted you. I knew by just getting to look up at you from down below, you had to have the biggest fucking dick this side of the Mississippi, and I guess I must have been right! Damn man, I've wanted something like this in my mouth ever since I was in the Army and looking at all the big thick dicks in the barracks! I did it with some of the white guys, but I never got to do one of the black studs, and you are the man like I've dreamed about sucking on, for years now! I think in the Army, all the black guys stuck together and did each other. I sure tried a number of times to let some of 'em know I was game! But I never got any of 'em, so now I really wanted you! I want that down my throat again, and then I wanna feel it up in my ass! I gotta know I took that damn big think up in me! I gotta! I've never been fucked before, and I want you to do me. Will you? You fuck guys?"

"Hell yeah I fuck guys! That's why I'm working here at this complex. It's got more hungry holes living here than any other apartment complex in the city."

"But, —the ring? You're wearing a wedding ring! You married, —I assume?"

"Yeah, I'm married, and so are you, —right? Barbara's not some live in girlfriend, right?"

"Yeah, I'm married. No she's not a live in, she my wife."

"So just how often do you use some guy instead of her?"

"Well, not too much anymore. Well, that was till I saw you and saw that enormous bulge sticking out the front of you! It's been a couple of years, till this morning, that is! Now, after getting to suck on this, and hopefully after getting to feel it up inside of my ole ass hole, I'll probably be back to trying to get it as often as I can. You're married, I'm married, guess that kinda screws up our getting together very often don't it?"

"Why you say that? Meaning, nowhere to meet and screw each other?"

"Well yeah! I sure can't let Barbara know I'm doing this stuff, and I guess you don't let you wife know either, right?"

"Yeah right, but we've always got apartment 117 available to us."

"What? What do you mean, apartment 117? Is it an empty apartment or something?"

"No, not an empty apartment, but Sam and Jim let me use it whenever I've got me a man I need to either get it from, or give it to. When I ran back over to the maintenance shop to get these rather needless washers, I called Jim and told him what was going on over here. See, I kinda knew you were wanting to play, and he told me to send you over to them, whenever you need action. He knows who you are, cause of your security uniform, and he said he'd love to do you. We can meet there whenever we need to, or want to. Hey guy, we could get ourselves a good four way going with those two guys! They know how to do the gay stuff! There good!"

Still kneeling down in front of Jack, and of course still right in front of Jack's big dick, Stan was looking up at Jack and listening to what he was saying. He then interjected. "Hey, you gotta tell those guys to quit watching for the security uniform now. I won't be wearing it anymore!"

"Why? Looks damn good on that hot muscle body of yours man. You change jobs, or something?"

"Yeah, finally! Tell 'em to start watching for a cop's uniform! I finally got accepted into the city police force. I'm in training right now, and I'll be a full blown cop shortly. I'll be wearing a policeman's uniform now."

"Well congratulations man, congrads! Good going! But, wait! Moment ago, you said you're gonna be a full blown cop! I think maybe then it's my responsibility right now to make sure your term, full blown, is right! Come on man, stand up here and let me down there and suck you off again, so you can really tell all your cop buddies you really are a full blown cop! Jerking off ain't really getting full blown, so come on, we need to graduate you to full blown status!"

Jack grabbed Stan by the arm pits and pulled him up, and he then immediately knelt down and took the future cop's dick into his mouth!

Grabbing Stan by the hips, Jack pulled him forward and ate all of his dick, immediately. Slamming his face forward and also pulling Stan's hips back and forth, did not give Stan any chance of holding off on another climax.

"Oh man, oh man, I'm gonna cum Jack!! I'm gonna cum! Oh shit man, I didn't think I'd cum this fucking fast again, oh man, here I cummmm man, —I'm cummmmmm!!! Oh shit man, that was good, oh yeah, I liked that! Oh Jack it's been years since I shot off in some guy's mouth! Oh man, that was good! Oh shit man, I forgot how hot a guy's mouth can be! Oh shit man, thanks! Thanks, —god that was good, —oh, fucking good!"

Licking his lips as he stood back up and pulled Stan up against himself, Jack asked, "So, been some time since you did this stuff right? My crotch got you all hot and bothered, uh? Liked the looks of it, I guess, —right?"

"Oh yeah man, hell yes! Barbara and I were together when I saw that and I think she saw me looking up at it! She made some remark and I just brushed it off, as just wondering who was working on the sign. I don't think I covered my tracks very good though. I've watched for you every day since then! I've seen you a number of times, but never when I could talk to you. Course, I knew damn well I was really taking my chances if I said the wrong thing, but this morning, I just had to have you, I did!"

"You bent that piece in the toilet, didn't you? It didn't leak before you saw me this morning did it?"

"No, hell no! I did that, and I knew for a couple of weeks what I was gonna do when I got the chance. I've been planning this little session for some time now. I just needed to find the right time, and when I saw you coming down the walk from the parking lot, I knew the time had come. I swear your crotch was standing out farther this morning than it was that day up on the ladder."

But Stan, what if my attitude had been a little different when I came in and you were purposely jerking off for me? What if I'd gotten all pissed off?"

"Then I'd have just asked you why in the hell did you need to go get washers, when I knew damn well the toilet didn't need washers! Hell man, you didn't need washers. All you wanted was to find out if it was just you and me here today, and you wanted to give me a chance to either hit the bed, all stretched out naked and hard, or maybe what I did, and that was hit the shower. I mean after all, you'd be in the bathroom, and so would I! And me, —all nice and naked! Gotta be honest with you though! I didn't think about the jerking off part, till I heard you opening up the front door, and all of a sudden, I thought, —hey man! Jerk off right in front of him, then he'll automatically know I'm game and that I'm anxious game! I figured that if I jerked it off right in front of you, that'd make it harder than it's probably been in years. Showed I was game didn't it? Worked, didn't it?"

"Hell yeah man, sure as shit did! Gotta admit that!"

"I didn't have any idea if you'd accept the idea of us doing something or not, —or maybe just beat the hell out of me whenever I approached you, but after I let you in the front door this morning, I knew I had a chance! I saw you looking down at my crotch, and you never so much as attempted any change of expression, but I saw a real slight grin! I knew damn well right then, that I had a chance. And don't try and tell me you didn't see that full hard on I had when I stepped out in the hallway to tell you to just come on in when you get back. I wanted you to see that, and I saw you looking! You smiled when you saw it. Hell man, I could have just yelled to you from the bedroom. I didn't really need to come out in the hall! I had a boner for you, and you damn well knew it! Come on man, give me some more of that fucking telephone pole that you call your dick! Fuck my mouth again! Let me have it. Give all of it to men, and give me your juices too! I can't go on the police force and know I've never tasted a black man's cum. Fuck my face!"

"OK, but how much time you got? I wanna fuck that tight little ass of yours before we're done."

"Hey I want you to, too, but how much time have you got? Is the office gonna wonder where you are?"

They don't open till nine on Saturdays, so I've got about 45 minutes yet. Then I'll have to get back to work, so come on, suck on me for a minute, make me shoot my wad in you, and then turn around there and let me drill you like I did when I was a kid and I was working on the knothole of some fence!"

"Oh god man, you gonna fuck me standing up? Can you do that?"

"Well, I know damn well I can do that, but the question might be, can you take it that way. Come on, suck me off, then we'll find out!"

"Jack, Jack did you really fuck knotholes when you were a kid? Did you really do that or was that a joke?"

"Not a joke man, —not a joke! But, —had to be big knotholes! Big holes! Think your hole's big enough?"

"Oh god I don't know, but I've gotta find out! Jack, I've gotta know I can take you up in there!"

"Ok then! Suck me off so we can find out just how much you can take up in there! You're gonna be a cop! You need to know you can take any fucking, that any guy down at the station, wants to give you! Come on, suck me off, we got work to do!"

CHAPTER NINE:

You Sure Those Two Guys Will Do That?"

"Oh God Stan, that feels so fucking good! Good man, good! Hell man, if it's been some time since you've eaten some guy's rod, you sure as hell remember how to do it! Suck it man, suck it! Come on man, make me blow my wad, I wanna use that ass hole of yours like I use to use the knotholes in the fence. I ain't fucked some ass standing up for a long time, and I wanna do that today! Yeah man, yeah, suck on it! Swallow that pole! Yeah man, yeah, take it deep! Come on man, you're getting me close, you're really doing me! Yeah, suck it, suck it! Come on make me flood your throat with my juice! Yeah, oh yeah Stan, you're doing it man, your doing it! Come on, —suck hard, real hard! Yeah, get ready for me, get ready! You're gonna get a mouth full when it explodes, and it's getting close, —it's getting close! Oh Stan, get ready man, get ready! Oh man—oh yeah, —oh yeah, —here it comes,—here it commmmes! Oh shit man! Damn man! Oh crap man that was good! Oh Stan, suck it dry, suck it dry! Oh man! Hey you are gonna be one good sucking cop man, one good sucking cop! Oh Stan, —yeah man, —yeah! Wow! Boy, oh boy! That sure as the hell took it out of me! Lick it clean man, can you lick it clean?"

Looking up at Jack, smiling and at the same time licking cum from his lips, the extra cum that just didn't fit into his mouth, Stan laid his head up against Jack's crotch and slightly licked the top of his dick and the fuzzy bush surrounding it. Slowly he lowered his face down and under Jack's bag of nuts, and lovingly, sucked Jack's left cum nut into his mouth.

"Oh yes man, oh yes!" Jack expounded with pleasure as he felt his nut slip and slide into Stan's mouth. "Oh man, suck it, —suck it, —suck it! Suck it hard! Yeah man, that's good, that's good!"

As Jack was almost yelling for Stan to suck on his nut, Stan then opened his mouth up wider and sucked in the right nut. He had a mouth full, and had to be very careful that he did not bite one of the nuts, too strongly, all in accident.

"Oh Stan, that's good! That's real good! Yeah man, yeah! Do that! Yeah, bite on 'em, bite on 'em! Oh Stan, I love that! Man, you sure as hell know how to make a man happy, especially if you ain't done this lately! Man, you must have been hungry for this, weren't you?"

Gently moving back, Stan continued to hug Jack's massive legs, but did allow Jack's nuts to slide out of his mouth, one at a time. He looked up at Jack and said, "I'm living the wrong life man, —I am! I know I am! Jack, I've forced myself to stay away from guys for years now, and I've wanted to feel some guy's dick pushed down in my throat and have him load me full, like you just did, —for years now! Oh Jack, I should've been doing this all along! Oh man, you are making me feel so fucking good! Come on man, I gotta feel that telephone pole or yours going up in my ass! I gotta take that man, I gotta take that! Freddie, one of my old army buddies that I never got to do anything with, was hung like you are, and I've dreamt of wanting to get that one up in my ass for years now, and now I'm gonna get yours and take yours! Put that thing up in me, —but if I call you

Freddie, I don't mean it, but I'll probably close my eyes and make believe it's his big black sausage that I'm finally, finally, getting. I've gone to sleep dreaming about wanting his dick going up in my ass for so many years now! I just can't believe I'm finally getting one that looks like his did! Hey Jack, if I call you the wrong name, I'm sorry, but I've wanted Freddie's big dick up in my ass and for it to fuck my ass for so long now, I know I'm gonna think it's his dick going up in me! Do me man, do me! Ram my ass with this fucking big thing! I want it, I want it! Oh gawd it is so big and pretty! It's like a hunk of gold!"

As Stan finished begging for Jack to fuck his ass, he lowered his face down and kissed both sides of Jack's big meat stick. Jack reached down and lifted Stan up by the arm pits, and told him, "Hey guy, stand up against the shower wall there. Lean on the wall. I've got me a small tube of KY lube in the bottom of my tool kit, and I'm gonna grab it and push some up in that tight ass of yours, so you can take my dick and make believe it's Freddie back here, drilling you a new ass hole with his big black rod!"

Turning his head slightly, Stan asked, "You've got KY lube in your tool box? You kidding man, you kidding?"

"No, I'm not kidding. I've got it! Hey, like I told you earlier, the reason I'm working here at this complex is the number of hungry ass holes that're walking around here, and a good maintenance man always comes prepared."

As Stan was getting his ass plugged with a good supply of KY he asked, "You serious man? There a lot of guys around here that play with each other?"

Leaning into Stan, and sliding some KY up into his ass, using two fingers so he could also slightly start to open Stan's chute, Jack replied! "Well man, on my list of playmates, you're gonna make the baker's dozen. In the short time I've been here, I've already got personal notes on twelve guys, and so you are gonna make number thirteen, the baker's dozen! If you're gonna be a gay friendly active cop, you sure are living in the right apartment complex. I'm kind of thinking there's more gay guys living in this complex than the rest of the town's got all over, anywhere else. And if you're not aware of it yet, I'm sure every gay guy around here has wet the front of his jeans by just watching you walking through, with your tight uniform pants on, and the ass of those pants kissing that tight ass of yours and the front hugging and kissing that big dick that shows so well. Hell man, when I told Jim that the security guy was making moves for me, he knew immediately which guy I was talking about. He wants you, and he wants you badly! You're gonna have to play with Jimmy and Sammy. They'll eat you up! They're both hot and fun! I think it's kinda funny that all you guys were living around each other and none of you knew about the other guy, until I came along, and now everybody's finding out about all the other players that they could have been doing, if they had only known."

"Oh Jack, I can feel your fingers up in there! Oh man, that is feeling so good! Yeah man, move 'em around up in there! Yeah man, put another finger up in there! Poke my hole with your fingers, yeah! Yeah-push up in there! Yeah man, I like that, —that feels good! Oh yeah, —poke me man, yeah poke me, —poke me, —poke me!"

"Hang tight man, hand tight! Think maybe my fingers have done what I wanted! Here comes the little hot dog you've been begging for! Ready? Ready to close your eyes and make believe your ole army buddy Freddie is moving in on you? Just think, it's gonna be just like ole Freddie doing you and your tight ass!"

"Oh yeah, yeah! But it sure as hell can't be called some little hot dog! More like a fucking steer dick on some fucking ragging bull! Oh man, do it! Do me! Yeah, I've gotta take this and I want this! Oh man, feed me, —feed me! Poke my hole! Push it up in me! Yeah, yeah! Oh Jack—oh Jack! Yeah man-yeah! Oh god all mighty man, —that is feeling so fucking good! Oh I feel like my ass is so fucking full! Oh yeah rip my ass and make me feel it! Do it man, do it! Yeah-push it in me, push it up in me! Oh Jack, this is great, this is fucking great! Oh Jack, put all of it in me! Push it in me hard! Yeah-slam my ass, slam my ass! Oh fill me up, fill me up! Oh Jack, I love this! I love this! Oh shit man, this is great, this is great! Oh shit I wish I could have talked old Freddie onto doing this to me back when I was in the

Army! I wanted him to fuck me so badly, I did! Oh man, this is great! Yeah—oh yeah! Oh yeah —poke my hole —poke my hole —poke my hole!! Slam my ass! Drill me man, drill me! Oh Jack, —Jack this is better than anything that I've ever done! Oh man, oh Jack, — poke me, —poke me! Hard!"

"Stan my man, I'm doing everything back here I can do! I swear man, I think I've even gotten my dick to stretch out about another inch or more trying to give you everything you want! You took that pole without so much as a whimper. Man your ass has been needing this for a hell of a long time, I can tell. I've never gone up and in some guy's ass that fast, that far before! Especially an ass that's not been fucked recently! Shit man, that ass of yours was standing open like the sewer line out on the street! Why in the hell did I ever think you needed some lube up in there? Hell man, I could have stuck my head up in there and I'm sure it would have fit! Man, your ass was on its hands and knees begging for that! Stan, did you know you were that fucking anxious to get rammed that hard and that deep back here?"

As Stan continued to stand there, leaning on the shower wall with his hands up toward the ceiling, and his ass pushing back, continuing to beg for more stiff, thick, muscular, action, he replied, "Jack, I knew before I called the office that I wanted to do some playing around with you, well obviously since I kinda set this whole thing up, but after I started to remembering Freddie and how I had prayed and prayed for years of wishing he would have poked me, then I just lost it man, I lost it! My ass could have taken an eighteen wheeler up in there right then. I've wished for years and years that Freddie would have fucked me, and today, I finally got it, and actually I think I got it from a bigger cock than Freddie had! One hell of a lot thicker, I know that for damn sure! Your dick is like a big fat zucchini squash! Damn man it felt good! Fucking good!"

"Well let me tell you something young man, —your ass can take it! Right now I think if I had a baseball bat handy, you'd be begging for that up in there! How you feeling? Feeling OK?"

"Yeah, I'm okay, but I want some more! Hey, can we like lay down out there on the hallway floor and pump me some more? I wanna feel you laying down on me! I wanna feel all of you laying on top of me and feel all your muscles rubbing on me. I wanna feel your body all over me! Can we, please, do you mind?"

"Hell yeah we can man. If that's what you want to do, of course, yes we can! Here, let's take these towels and spread 'em out so we don't get the floor too wet, and come on, —let's do it!"

Stand and Jack grabbed a couple of towels, slightly dried themselves, then spread the towels out on the floor in the hallway, and Stan immediately laid down and spread his legs, showing once again that he was anxious and hungry to feel Jack's thick, long, stiff male shaft going back up inside of himself.

"Hey man, ready? Ready to take this thing again?" Jack asked as he laid down on Stan's back and gently and lovingly started to slip his eleven incher up, and into Stan's ass. He slowly laid himself down and drove himself up into Stan, as he once again took possession of that tight little white ass that he had just so feverously rammed the hell out of while standing in the shower. After the slow and loving entry, and his hugging Stan around his chest, so that Stand could feel all of his muscles laying on his back like he had asked for and said he wanted, Jack then actually started ramming his rod up and into Stan, without waiting for an answer to his question of if he was ready or not. Jack knew that as hungry and anxious as Stan was for his dick, he was ready! He was ready, he was anxious, he wanted it, and he wanted it badly!"

"Oh Jack, do me, do me! Oh man your dick up in there is so fucking good! Oh man, ram my ass, ram me! Give me your dick! Give it to me, make me know I've got all of you up in me! Oh Jack, oh man, we gotta do this all the time! I'm serious man, I'm gonna need this all the time! I love this!"

"Hey Stan my man, you are gonna get it all the time! I'm gonna make sure you do man, I'm gonna make sure you do! I'm gonna be the man that gets to take your new policeman uniform off of you and fuck your ass while you lay there and bury your face in those policeman pants, aren't I? I'm gonna be the man that gets to fuck you the night you become a full fledged policeman, right? You gonna let me do that man? Do I get to fuck my cop that night?"

"Oh yes man, oh yes! Oh Jack, that sounds so fucking hot to me man, oh yes you can! Oh yeah, I'll lay there and put my nose in the crotch of my police pants and let you put your dick up in me while I lay there and sniff my own pants! Oh Jack, oh god man, that sounds so fucking hot to me, yeah-we gotta do that!"

"Oh tell you what Stan man, tell you what!" Jack whispered into Stan's ear as he pounded his ass and at the same time made mad passionate love to all of Stan's body, not only his ass. "Tell you what I think we ought to do. I think Jimmy, Sammy and I should come to your academy graduation ceremony, and just sit there as if we were long time friends, and let you look at us, knowing that later that night after all the celebrating, we're all gonna be fucking you and your new policeman's ass! Hey, what do you think about that? Like that? Wanna stand up there and look out at us knowing that before the night is over, all three of us guys are gonna take care of that new cop ass? Like that?"

"Oh my god Jack, oh shit! Oh Jack that is turning me on man, that is so fucking hot! Jack, I'd be up there, on the stage with everybody sitting there, watching me graduate and I'd know that you three guys were all gonna be fucking my ass yet that same night! Oh Jack, —Barbara and both of my parents are gonna be there too, and we'd have this big, big secret of what's really gonna happen to me and my ass later that night! Oh Jack fuck my ass, fuck me hard! That idea has got me just about crazy, just thinking about it! Oh man, I'd just wanna stand up there and yell out, 'Those three guys are gonna fuck me when this is over!' Oh Jack, you think Jimmy and Sammy would do that? We could use their place, right? Oh god man, that is turning me on like shit! Oh god man, I wish that was today! Oh man, that is so fucking hot to just think about! I'm gonna have to tell Barbara that all of the new grads are having a get together so I can get out for long enough to get it three or four times that night! Oh shit man, oh shit! Damn I wanna do it now! "

"Yeah man, just think! You standing up there on the stage, being the center of attention, you in your nice new tight fitting policeman pants, and when you look out and see us three with our anxious dicks looking up at you, your ole boner starts showing right through those cop pants! Oh man, I'd love to see that happen, I'd love that! I can see the newspaper the next day, —headlines say, "New cop shows the city he's got a big dick, right there on the graduation stage!" Yeah, I want you to have a hard on when you graduate man, I do! I wanna sit out there in the audience and watch your dick get hard in those tight pants! Oh shit man, I hope that happens! I hope like hell it does! Oh god man, I gotta take a camera with me so I can take a picture of you standing there, showing the whole world your big stiff cop hard on!"

"Oh fuck me, fuck me! Jack, pound me hard! If you have to man, take your dick off and leave it up inside of me! Make me have it man, make me have it! You've got me so fucking hot, I won't be able to do anything until that day except think about that happening! Oh Jack, you sure Jimmy and that Sammy will do that? Oh man, just thinking I'll be standing there with Barbara and my Mom and Dad looking at me, and I'll be knowing that you three guys are there, in the same room, and you're gonna be fucking my ass like crazy in just a little while! Oh man, what in the hell will I do if I do get a hard on? What in the hell would I do? I know damn well it will show through those pants if I get hard! Oh man, what in the hell am I gonna do if I do get hard? Oh man, oh shit, I never thought I'd ever be thinking about something like that! Oh shit man, I can't wait! You sure those two guys will do that? Just knowing that I've got three guys, sitting there, watching the graduation, and you're in there waiting on me, so you can take me home and fuck my ass! What a fucking turn on that is! Oh shit man, what a fucking turn on! You sure those two guys will do that?"

"Oh yeah, oh yeah! Oh hell yeah man, hell yeah! Hey, Jimmy already told me this morning how he wanted me to tell you to just go find apartment number 117 whenever you needed some action, so hell yes, I know they will! They like to play with guys and you'll like playing with them! We'll fuck the hell out of you that night so that you know you can take whatever those other cops wanna give you some night, —when you're out on late night patrol! Cops love to fuck other cops, and man, with the tight little muscle body on you, and this tight little ass I'm pounding the hell out of right now, you are gonna be good hunk of meat for them guys! You just gotta remember that whenever you find out which of your buddies is game, you gotta get me with 'em. I love cop ass and I ain't had any for way too long! I need to know I've got me a couple of the city's finest available to me! You're gonna be a big help to me man, a big help! White cops love black asses and black dicks, so you gotta help me let 'em know I'm their man whenever they get hungry for black!"

"Oh Jack, why in the hell would I let them know about you when I know damn well I'm gonna need this all the time myself! Oh Jack, make me feel your dick way up in my throat! Jack push that thing up in me so it comes out of my throat! Oh fuck me, —fuck me, —fuck me!!!"

"Hey, hon, I am, and from the way I'm starting to feel right now, you're just about to get another load up in you! You ready to get bred again man? You ready? I'm getting damn close! Oh Stan, I'm gonna do you man, I'm gonna do you! Hang on, hang on! Oh Stan, —oh Stan here it comes, —I'm cumin man, —I'm cumin man! Oh shit your ass feels so fucking good! Damn you've got a good ass! Oh Stan your ass is unbelievable man, —totally unbelievable, —totally unbelievable! Oh shit, what a fucking ass! Damn man, oh God I hope I can get some work done today! Oh Stan, I love fucking this ass! Hey man, just think, —I'm gonna fuck it on your graduation night, right? Right? I get to be the first guy to fuck the new cop, right, —right?"

"Oh yeah man, Oh yes! Oh that idea has got me so fucking hot, —so fucking hot! Hey Jack, let me roll over and you suck my dick some, OK? My dick's wanting to cum and I need to watch you going down on it! Would you?"

"Hell yeah man, roll over! Let me have that dick! I love sucking on that dick! Oh yeah, I'm gonna suck on a new cop's dick! Yeah, I want this thing man, give it to me!"

"Oh Jack, yeah! Yeah suck me man, suck me! Oh Jack, I can feel your cum running out of my ass! Oh man, I can feel it! I can feel it!"

Jack pulled off of Stan's rod just long enough to look up at him and say, "Hey man, good thing we put those towels down then man, good thing!" He immediately took Stan's meat back into his mouth and sucked hard and strong!

"Oh Jack, I'm gonna cum man, I'm gonna cum! Here it comes man, I'm cumin, —I'm cummmmin! Oh suck me, my dick feel likes it's about twice the size it really is! Oh man, it feels so fucking big! Oh thanks man, thanks! Not only for this cum shot but for everything man, everything! I said earlier I'm living the wrong life, and I know now, damn well, I am! Oh man, I've needed this for a hell of a long time! Oh Jack, please tell me we will be doing this all the time! Please promise me this will only be the first of a lot of times! Oh I love feeling you and having you up inside of me! Jack, —thanks man, thanks! You're my fucker man, you're my fucker! I love this! Oh Jack, I wish Freddie would have done this to me years ago! I wish he had. My whole life would be different right now, I know damn well it would've been!"

"Well Stan. Did Freddie play with any guys that you know of? Did he play around with guys?"

"You know, I don't know! I really don't! He was such a hot stud, he could have, whenever he wanted to, and with any guy or gal he wanted to, but I was a puny little guy back then, and I know I sure didn't turn him on any, so I just don't know. I saw him and some of the other big hunky guys goofing around with each other, but just like grabbing or wrestling with each other, but I never saw him having any kind of sex with 'em. I tried every way I could think of to get him to do me, but I guess I sure wasn't the right one for him! The whole time we were on the same base, I wanted him to just grab me, if nothing else! I wanted him to feel me, so I could feel him. I just wanted to feel his hands on me someplace, anyplace! I just wanted to know he had touched me, someplace! It's all cause of Freddie that I spent the thousand and thousand of hours working out in the weight room so that I could finally get me a playmate and have sex with a man like him, —well, like you! Jack, I've had a hard on for you, ever since that first day I saw you! Today was finally my payoff day, and damn it, it was worth it man, totally worth it!"

"Stan, —if you're built like you are all because of that Freddie guy, you owe him a lot! You are one hot tight muscled man, and you look good! Fucking good! Maybe it's better that Freddie never did you! If he'd had done you, you would never have built yourself up to be the little god you are! Today, you can get any guy you want, and you are gonna be one hot looking cop. You're gonna be what all the gay guys are wanting, so just know that whenever you want it or need it, you're gonna have a line of guys wanting it, and wanting it from you, —like you wanted from Freddie! You're hot man, real hot! Fucking hot!"

"Thanks man, thanks! That's good coming from someone that's built like you, and of course hung like you! Come on, let's shower down and get cleaned up. It's just about nine o'clock, and I want you to call that Jimmy and Sammy and see if maybe you and I can stop in their place today sometime, so I can meet 'em. Will you? Can you? Oh yeah, maybe we can ask them if they'll come to the graduation ceremony and kinda make sure that's all gonna work out, —OK?"

"Yeah, sounds like a good idea. Hey, tell you what. I'll call Jimmy and just tell him you and I wanna come over there for lunch! He'll be more than glad to feed us lunch, and anything else that happens to, —come up!"

"Oh Jack, that sounds good, that's great! I'm anxious to meet 'em."

And with a very big grin on his face, Stan added, "Oh yeah, also, thanks for fixing the toilet! I hope it breaks again! I've never met a maintenance man just quite like you! Hell man, I don't think there are any others quite like you! You got one hell of a fucking tool just hanging on you! What a fucking muscle man you are. You're the first guy I've done anything with in years, my first muscle guy, and of course my first black man. What a prize man, what a prize! And of course you damn well know that's the first time I've even seen an eleven inch dick! What a fucker, —what a fucker you are! Down my throat and up my ass, both! Damn man, —thanks, —you are good! You sure as the hell have changed my life for me! And I'm sure I'm not the first one, and sure as hell won't be the last one, either! Right?"

CHAPTER TEN:

You Serious man, You Serious?

"Ray, Ray, — come here Ray!" Bret was almost screaming as he came barreling in though the front door.

"Ray, look at that! Look!" Bret was exclaiming as he pointed out the front window and looked down toward the man walking across the courtyard below.

"Who in the hell is that? Whoa, Bret, — who in the hell is that?"

"That's the new maintenance man! That's who that is! What in the hell do you think of that?"

"Oh shit man, shit! He is fucking hot! You sure he's the new guy?"

"Yeah, I am. He's got the uniform shirt on with the apartment logo on one side and his name on the other side. The apartment newspaper said last month we had a new maintenance man, but they sure as hell never said he was a God of a man, —directly from heaven. God is he built!"

"Bret did you talk to him? Have you met him yet?"

"No, all I did was walk past him and we both just kind of nodded and said 'Hi." Of course I was fighting to keep from fainting when I got close to him. Look at those shorts he's got on. Man, oh man! They're hugging that tight ass of his like some of that plastic shrink wrap stuff they wrap meat in on the meat counter. God I wish his ass was laying on our meat counter!"

"God yeah man, —those are hot as hell, —but I've never seen some maintenance guy that wears shorts like that, have you?"

"No I haven't, but who in the hell cares, now!? Man, when you're built like that and have legs like that, fuck man, as far as I'm concerned, he could run around naked and I don't think anybody would bitch. I know that if he was out there naked, I'd be out there trying to eat him up! Damn he's hot!"

"Those shorts just look kind of like they were originally some uniform pants that were cut off and cuffed, don't they?"

"Yes and my God man do they fit that ass tight! Hey, what'd they look like in the front? You were walking toward him right? What's the front look like?"

"The front looks like it's trying to hide about two feet of dick! Honestly man, what a fucking basket he has got! And oh yeah —of course, a wedding ring!"

"Oh shit man, —you're kidding right? You are kidding, aren't you?"

"No I'm not! No, — he's definitely got a wedding ring on. The two things I saw when I was walking toward him was the enormous basket from hell and the wedding ring."

"Well Bret, — when you guys got kind of close to each other, how did he act? Was he friendly?"

"Yeah, —yeah he was friendly. I mean he didn't like grab hold of me and give me a big kiss or anything like that, but he didn't ignore me either! He was nice."

"You were wishing he would have grabbed ahold of you, weren't you? Hell man, I don't blame you at all! Oh shit man, we have got to get him up here and do some work on something. I've got to see that guy up close! Oh Bret, what do we need done?"

"That drain under the kitchen sink is still dripping a little, and I'm sure we could use that as our excuse if you want to. I mean, it don't drip too much, but hey, if we tell the office we've got a drip, it's no lie. Hell, just seeing him walking around down there is making me drip like some fucking gay whore anyway!"

"Fuck man, you sure ain't the only one! Honestly man, I have not seen anything that hot looking for a hell of a long time."

"Well, thanks man, —thanks!" Bret responded, with a large fake frown on his face.

"Hey honey, I'm sorry. I didn't mean you aren't hot, you are hot, damn hot, but you've got to admit that those legs and that butt, and then of course that chest and those arms, oh crap the whole fucking thing is hotter than all of us normal guys wrapped together!"

"Ok, —so you gonna call the office and tell them we've got a leak up here?"

"Yeah, yeah, I am. I want that guy in here working on something just so I can see him up close! Dam man, he makes me weak!"

Ray looked at Bret as if to silently ask, "OK?" and, as he got a grin from Bret, he dialed the apartment office.

"Hello, this is Ray Norton in apartment 312. The drain pipe under the kitchen sink is dripping, well, — has been for some time now, and I've been keeping a pan under it to catch the water. Can you have someone come up and look at it for us? —Great, yeah we'll be here all afternoon, so if possible I sure do appreciate it!"

Ray hung up the phone, turned toward Bret and said, "The gal in the office said that somebody, —man, — she better be talking about that hunky black man, could come up in just a little while. I told her we've been using a pan under there to catch the drips. I've got to go put a pan under there and just put a little water in it so that I don't look like I'm lying incase they tell him I said that."

"OK guy! So now that you've hopefully got him headed this way, you gonna try and dress yourself real sexy looking so that you look good too?"

"Hey man, gotta do whatever a guy's gotta do, you know!" Ray replied as he headed for the kitchen to set up his fake drip pan, and then quickly down the hall to put on some of his sexiest shorts and a tank top.

Bret and Ray were, in their own rights, two very attractive men and lovers that had been together for the past five years. Bret was aged 37 and Ray was a year younger at age 36. Both men were very active in the local health and gym club, always attempting to build the type of a body that they had both been so hungrily, lusting over as they watched Jack just simply walk across the apartment property. The sight of a good, well defined and very muscular male body had always turned each of them on, and they had, in fact, originally met at the health club. Each man was very well aware that his partner always had the hots for any hot, well built man, and one that even slightly looked anything like Jack, was a major excitement for both of them.

"Hi, I'm Jack Jensen, the maintenance man. This is apartment number 312 isn't it? Are you Ray Norton? I understand you have a leaking drain problem somewhere here in your apartment, right?"

"Yeah we do. Yeah, Jack. Come on in."

Jack entered the apartment, walked past Ray, as Ray closed the front door, and then happened to see Bret as he was coming out of the kitchen and headed toward the living room area.

"Oh! Hi!" Jack spoke as he saw Bret. "Hey, saw you earlier this afternoon didn't I? You were down on the courtyard earlier, weren't you?"

"Yeah, I was. Yeah we kind of passed each other when I was headed back here from the mail box. I'm Bret." Bret extended his hand out to shake hands with Jack as he continued, "We kind of said Hi, but we never actually met!"

Jack and Bret shook hands as Jack then asked, "Is the drain problem in the kitchen or in the bathroom?"

In a rather confused moment, Bret and Ray both, at the same time, replied, "Oh, in the kitchen!"

As they went into the kitchen area, Ray quickly apologized that he had not taken the stuff out from under the sink and asked for just a moment to get it emptied so that Jack could get in there and work on the drain.

As Ray was sitting on the floor after quickly taking everything out from under the sink, he turned to start to get up, and discovered that he was directly "face to face" with Jack's crotch. He did not realize that Jack was standing quite so closely as he was. Without meaning to, he suddenly uttered an "Oh my God!" as he turned and suddenly saw the tight covered crotch that was so close to his face. Jack rather jumped back ever so slightly and said, "Oh, I'm sorry! I didn't mean to crowd you!"

"Oh that's OK." Ray managed to say as he started to realize that he was truly taking way too much time in managing to remove himself for this close proximity to the hidden dick, —the dick that he truly did want to see! As he managed to get up from on the floor, he looked back and saw Bret standing there with his mouth hanging open, as he was silently admiring the back side of what Ray had so unexpectedly been confronted with on the other side. As Ray looked at Bret, Bret ever so slightly shook his head as in complete disbelief.

Jack put his tool box down on the floor close to where he then laid down and scooted up and under the sink. Then, just as he rather got positioned, he looked back toward Ray and Bret and asked, "Hey Ray. Have you got maybe a bath towel that we can put down here on the floor of the cabinet so that if any water drips out, the towel will catch it instead of getting the floor wet?"

"Oh yeah! Yeah let me get one." Ray quickly replied, as he headed out of the kitchen and into the hall to get a towel from the storage cabinet.

Returning to the kitchen, he offered it to Jack, but Jack then suggested, "Hey Ray, can you kinda spread it out under me some? Here, slide it up and under here. Yeah guy, yeah."

Rather than slide back out of the cabinet, Jack rather stood his ground of where he was, and thus encouraged Ray to get down and kind of into the cabinet with him, to spread out the towel, the best he could.

As Ray attempted to spread the towel the best he could, he wondered for a moment if it wouldn't have been easier if Jack had just gotten back out of the cabinet and then spread the towel, that is until, all of a sudden he realized that Jack was reaching over the top of him to grab onto the corner of the towel and pull it up and into place.

"Hey Ray, hope you don't mind me kinda crowding you some, but I needed to pull this up and in place."

Ray was now rather pinned in place with Jack having his arm out and across his torso, and his chest rather up close and tight to Ray's chest. He looked at Jack, directly in his face, and saw Jack break into a slight grin.

Ever so slightly, Jack winked at Ray, then said, "Hey thanks man. That oughta do it." And as he told Ray thanks, Ray noticed that as Jack's arm was removed from across his body, it rather smoothly dropped down so that Jack's left hand just happened to land on his own crotch. Jack watched Ray's eyes, and as he watched Ray glance down and see Jack's hand hit his basket area, Jack asked. "Hey guy, wanna hold this wrench in place for me so I can try and get this drain taken apart?"

With both men now positioned in rather tight and close quarters under the kitchen sink, Ray was definitely convinced that it really was not necessary for him to be crammed in there to hold any wrench. Once again he looked at Jack's face, and once again he saw Jack break out in a slight grin, and give him another slight wink.

"You Ok with helping me with this?" Jack asked of Ray.

"Yeah, yeah! I am if you need me. Yeah it's Ok." Ray replied.

With that reply, Jack responded. "Good! Here hold that wrench right there and let me see if I can get this to loosen up." Ray reached up as comfortably as he could to grab onto the wrench that Jack had asked him to hold, and at the same time, realized that Jack had reached back and had grabbed ahold of an additional wrench that was laying on the floor of the cabinet. As Jack brought the wrench forward, it was very obvious to Ray that Jack definitely, and on purpose, had let the back of his hand sweep across, and had actually stopped it and rested up against Ray's crotch, for just a second. Jack saw Ray glance down, and then back up, and looked at him directly in the face. Jack asked, "You OK?"

"Yeah, yeah. Yeah, I'm Ok, but maybe just a little confused here. That's all, just a little confused."

As Jack loosened the drain fitting, which did come loose rather easily, he asked, "Confused? Confused about what Ray?"

Still holding the wrench in place, Ray replied. "Well, uhh, I'm not sure, I guess! Uhh, you still need me to hold this wrench?"

Looking at Ray, grinning slightly, Jack answered, "Well, not really, but if you would, I'd appreciate it. OK? Everything OK?"

"Yeah, I guess so, but for some reason, I'm just not sure why I'm doing this. Don't seem like you really need me doing it."

"Hey Ray, tell you what! The faster we get this leak fixed, the more time I'll have to really get to know you and Bret. Understand?"

"Get to know me and Bret? Is that what you said? Is that right?"

"Yeah man, yeah! Ray, I saw you looking at my basket when you were getting the stuff out of the cabinet, and I also saw Bret looking at it when we said "Hi" to each other a little while ago. Ray, when that happened down on the sidewalk, I knew damn well right then, that I was gonna be up here fixing something this afternoon. At that time, I didn't know if both of you guys were home today or not, but I figured if it was only Bret, I'd be getting a call. Fact is, I went to the office and kinda goofed off doing some paper work just waiting for a phone call that I knew was gonna be coming in. And it did! And both of you guys are here, so this is going great for me! Now, let's get this damn thing fixed, whatever fixing it needs, and get out from in this little spot. OK? Game? Think Bret's gonna be game?"

"Jack, what do I say? Man, this is a shock! You saying you want to do something with us? Is that what you're saying?"

"Yeah man, that is what I'm saying! And looking at both of you guys, I'm anxious. Game?"

"Oh shit yeah man, yeah I'm game! Yeah, I know Bret's gonna be game too. Hell yeah, the way he was about to go faint from just saying 'Hi' to you earlier. Want me to tell him what's going on?"

"Naw, not yet! OK? Let's finish up under here, then we'll tell him, OK?"

"Yeah, Ok with me. But Jack! You're wearing a wedding ring! You're married aren't you?"

"Yeah, married, but getting a little pussy each night just ain't enough for me man, just ain't enough." Jack then explained to Ray his reasonings for taking this particular job, and told him about some of the great sessions he had already had with some of the other tenants.

Jack finished putting the drain pipe back together, looked at Ray, who was still under the sink with him, and said, "OK! It's together. Repaired! Well, we'll say it's repaired! OK? Really didn't leak enough to need a repair, did it?"

As Jack broke out in a broad grin as he asked Ray if it didn't really need any repair, Ray grinned back and admitted that, "No! We decided to call and say it was really leaking just in hopes of getting you up here. Bret is gonna be really shocked when we tell him what's up! That drain was leaking a just a little, but not enough to where we needed to put a pan under it. That was a set up. We faked how bad it was."

"So how we gonna let Bret know this little repair trip is changing course?"

"Hey, let me holler at him and tell him to come in here. He's in the back room on the computer. When he gets in here, I'll ask you to take your shirt off, and we'll let it go from there, OK?"

"Yeah, yeah!" Jack anxiously replied. "Yeah, let's do that!"

"Hey, Bret! Bret come into the kitchen. Jack said he's got the drain fixed."

As Bret came into the kitchen, he heard Ray saying, "Oh come on man, come on! Take your shirt off, please! Please, I wanna see your chest!"

Bret's mouth snapped open as he walked into the kitchen, heard Ray making the 'take your shirt off,' plea, and also seeing his partner Ray actually reaching forward and unbuttoning Jack's shirt.

"Hey guys! What in the hell is going on in here? Ray, what in the hell are you doing? Ray, what are you doing?"

Looking over his shoulder toward his partner, Ray answered. "Hey guy! Remember how hot you were for this guy when you saw him earlier down on the sidewalk, —well he's available, and we're gonna get to play with him! He just knew you were gonna call for some kind of a repair today after he saw you looking at his crotch. He told me that's why he took this job! He knew this place had a lot of gays living here. He told me he needs action with guys all the time, and he's been real anxious to meet us. He knew all about us, well anyway, enough to know we were gay guys! Come on man, help me get him stripped down. He told me he's game, and I wanna see this man without anything on! I wanna see this man naked, totally naked. This day is turning out one hell of a lot hotter than I expected. Come on Bret, —about an hour ago you were ready to rape him out on the sidewalk, well now we get to do him right in here!"

"Oh shit man, I can not believe this! I can't! Jack, you okay with this? This okay with you?"

"Hell yes man, hell yes! That's why I'm working here! It ain't for the pay, believe me man, it ain't for the pay! It's for the ass and the creamy stiff dicks around here! I knew earlier when I saw you dripping saliva down your chin when you looked at my basket that I needed to be ready and available cause I knew you were gonna have some kind of a problem up here, and here I am. Come on man, help your man get these clothes off of me, and you get stripped too! We're gonna do ourselves a major three way before I get out of here. Either one of you guys ever sucked on an eleven inch black cock before?"

And with that question, Bret let out with an, "Oh my God man, did you say eleven inches? Is that what you said?"

"Yeah man, yeah! Eleven, and if you get me a little more excited, it just might reach out and hit the ole magic twelve incher! Interested? Your mouth feeling kinda hungry for it?"

"Oh my God man, I ain't never had anything like that in my mouth before!" Bret again exclaimed as he looked over at his lover Ray and asked, "Ray! Ray, you ever tried something like that? You ever had something that big in your mouth before?"

"I tired it once with a banana once, and hell no, it did not go in! Jack, you serious, you gonna try to stick that down our throats?"

"Only if you guys wanna try it! I've got about maybe ten or twelve guys here at the complex that have done it so far, and I don't think any of them thought they could take it either, but guess what, —they did! Did, and then begged for more! The first two guys I got on it, were Jim and Sammy down at apartment 117. And now maybe about ten more, including the new cop. He's that hot looking stud that used to wear the guard uniform. The night that he graduated from the police academy, he and Jim and Sammy and I got together and the cop took it all the way, —even though he was sure he couldn't! I told him he had to take it so that if one of his buddy cops was a hung big black guy, he had to know he could do it, and by God, he can! Now he claims that he wants it all the time, like at least twice or three times a week. He's married, I'm married, and that's why Jim and Sammy's apartment is so important to us now. We need the space! But hey guys, with you two, —we don't have that problem! Your place! If you guys like it, want it, and need it, we don't need to go find a hideout place, do we? Come on guys, I wanna see what two hot guys like you two have got to offer the ole maintenance man!"

Standing there with his arms reaching up toward the ceiling, his feet spread apart and his tongue licking his lips, Jack let Bret and Ray open his shirt, unbuckle and then unbutton his shorts, and start to push 'em down just far enough to realize that Jack had no under briefs on with those short tight uniform shorts! He actually had his enormous rod tucked back in between his legs, so that it didn't fall down and out of the bottom of his shorts!

"Oh my God man!" Ray almost shouted out as he realized that Jack did not have any briefs on!

"My God man, how in the hell can you go around without any briefs on with a dick like that and those short shorts? How in the hell can you keep from letting it fall out?"

"Hey men, you just gotta know how to work the job! When I found out just who's apartment the call came from, into the back of my shop, —shorts down, —briefs off, —tuck the ole rod up and back in, and then put the shorts back on! I knew I was not gonna want any briefs on when I came over here! I was kinda hoping that maybe for some reason or another, one of you guys would want to just slide your hand up inside of 'em, and if you did, I sure wanted you to be able to just grab ahold of my dick and not have some stupid briefs in the way! I was hoping maybe that when I laid down on my back and slid in under the counter, one of you might just look at my legs and my crotch, and loose all of your self control and just reach up in there to see what was in there! Why wear stuff that gets in the way? I was hoping one of you would kinda reach up in there and grab that chocolate bar that's hidden up in there! I was really just hoping that one of you would just decide that you needed to grab whatever you could! Come on guys, pull those shorts down, I gotta dick that needs some tongue work on it! Who's gonna be first?"

Ray and Bret finished getting the hunk of the maintenance man all undressed, and he did the same for each of them. As he stripped each man naked from the waist down, he bent down, took a respective dick into his mouth, and after a few good strong vacuum sucks, stood up, licked his lips and with a very big grin on his face and stated, "Damn man, I found it today! Damn men, for two white dicks, those sure are good tasting dicks! I'm gonna need to come by here really often and check out this apartment and make sure everything is going okay! Yeah men, I am! Okay guys, now that I've gotten a nice little taste of what lives in apartment number 312, just who is gonna be the first one to take a small railroad car down his throat? I've got creamy stuff in there that I known needs to get out of there. Which one guys?"

As Ray and Bret rather stood there, both wondering just how in the hell either one of them was gonna be able to do it, Ray finally said, "Bret, you do it! You go first."

"Me!? Why me?" Bret rather strongly questioned, but with somewhat of a smile in his voice. He was not sounding like he was asking with fear in his voice, but with more of a "Thank you!"

"You, because look at that ass! You suck his dick, and I'm gonna suck that ass like he ain't never had it sucked before! Bret, look at those two thick solid hunks of beef back there! I'm gonna stick my face up in there and I'm gonna see if I can get my tongue up in that little hole of his to where he begs and begs for me to stick it in farther! I want that ass! Man, —do I want that ass! I wanna feel my face pushed up in there and feel both of those slabs of beef pushing up against the sides of my face as I'm pushing it in as far as I can get it to go! "

With that strong comment as to just why Ray wanted Bret to be the first one on Jack's big stick, Bret did not object. He knelt down in front of Jack, and with both hands, took ahold of what was now a big, thick, black, velvet pole standing so straight out, that Bret actually had to step back a full foot, just to approach the end of it. As he started down onto it, with his mouth forced open as far as it would go, just to get it around the thick stick of meat, and down onto it as far as he could right then, he saw his lover move into place and encourage Jack to grab ahold of each of his own ass cheeks to pull them apart, so that he could get his face up and in between those two hunks of solid ass muscle, just as far as possible! He was really pushing with his face!

One man was now on the front of Jack, chewing, sucking and licking, and the other man was up and in his ass, as far as he could get his face pushed. Ray was sucking, licking, and chewing on each and every piece of mahogany meat that he could get his mouth, this tongue or his teeth onto!

As Jack reached out toward the kitchen counter to steady himself, trying to push his ass out and back toward Ray, and at the same time push his dick into Bret's anxious and hungry mouth, he said, "Oh shit man, —oh god men, —this is great! Oh this feels so fucking good! Oh men do me, —do me! Bret, take it man, take it, all of it man, all of it! Oh shit Ray, lick it man, lick it! Stick your tongue up in there man, stick your tongue up in there! Oh men, this is better than I expected, —a hell of a lot better! Do it men, do it! Eat me out men, eat me out! Oh men, oh men! Oh guys this is even so much better than the other night when the four of us got together to celebrate Stan's graduation! Oh men, eat me men, eat me! Yeah, oh yeah, oh yeah! Do it men, —do it! Ray, bite my ass man, —bite my ass! Let me feel your teeth biting into me man, let me feel it! Oh Bret take it man, take it. Come on man, take it! Eat my dick man, eat my dick! Swallow it man, swallow it! Take it! Yeah man, yeah take it!"

Jack took turns between grabbing the back of Bret's head and helping him force his throat down onto his baseball bat of a dick, and also reaching back and pulling his ass apart so that Ray could force his face up and into his ass crack more and more. At one time, Jack did rearrange the three of them so that Ray's head was back against the cabinet door, and he could then push back against Ray's face, to force his ass onto Ray's face that much more.

"Yes, yes, yes, man! Yes, bite my ass! Ray make me feel your teeth man, let me feel your teeth biting me man, biting me! Oh man alive I love that, I love that! Yeah man bite, —bite! Oh I've never had a man bite on my ass hole like that before, I love that! That is so good, oh so fucking good! Yeah Ray, yeah! Yeah get right on the rose bud of my ass and bite it man, bite it! Oh yeah, oh yeah! Oh my god Bret, I'm gonna cum man, I'm gonna cum! Bret, get ready man, get ready, I'm gonna, oh man, here it cums man, here it cuuuuummmmmmmmmmms! Oh shit man, —oh shit! Oh guys, bite me, suck me, lick on me, oh men do it, this is so fucking good men, —this is the best sex I've had ever! Oh men, how in the hell can I thank you guys for what in the hell you have just done for me! Oh men, oh! Oh shit, let me lean on the counter guys, —I gotta lean here a minute! Oh what in the hell can I do to make this up to you guys? Oh shit that was great! Oh, what in the hell can I do?"

Pulling his face off of Jack's stick of steel, and licking the extra cum that was now sliding out of his mouth, Bret looked up at Jack and asked, "You serious man, you serious? You wanna know what you can do? You really asking?"

Looking down at Bret and still encouraging Ray to keep up the action in his ass, Jack answered, "Yeah man, yeah."

Resting back on his heels, a hand on each of Jack's strong muscled oak tree legs, and pushing Jack's still stiff hard on, back and forth with his face, Bret said, "You can pay us back by being here for at least one hour for the next ten days, and making sure that both of us get this big chocolate, thick, big veined black, stiff milk dud, and all of it's creamy white sauces up in our asses each time you are here. You gotta show up here each day and make a deposit in one or the other of us, or in both of us!" Then looking around toward Ray, he continued, "That Ok with you Ray?"

"Oh fucking yes man, fucking yes! Oh god man, hell yes! I want that thing up in my ass and I want it good and deep, and every day for at least the next ten days! I wanna see what it feels like to have something that big, that thick, that stiff, and that strong, blast off inside of me!"

"Got it men, got it! That's not really much of a pay off, since I'm probably more anxious to do that than you guys are, but hell yes! Next ten days, at least one hour each day, and in both asses as deep as it will go, and as forceful as I can squirt it, each time! This is heaven men, heaven! What a way to abuse my dick! Damn man, I like this! You gotta promise me though, that I'm gonna get my ass bud chewed on and bitten on some more like I got today, though. Agreed?"

With one hell of a smile on his face, Ray replied, "Oh yeah man, oh yeah! Any fucking part of that body you want played with, bitten on, or chewed on, you just let us know! You do for us, and we'll do for you!"

CHAPTER ELEVEN:

Sex With Her is Gonna Be Meaningless

"Hey Sam, there's the front door now!"

Jim jumped up from his spot on the couch, watching a good old showing of "The Golden Girls" and headed for the door.

Jim opened the door, and the man on the outside said, "Hi, I'm Chuck."

Jim obviously opened the screen door, extended his hand out for a hand shake, and replied, "Hi, I'm Jim Nelson, come on in."

Jim led Chuck into the living room and introduced him to Sam, suggested that he sit down, as Jim then did, and Jim asked, "So Chuck what's up? Jack, the maintenance guy called earlier today and told us that you were gonna stop by and talk to us, but other than that, we have no idea of what is going on. What's up?"

Chuck kind of hesitantly looked at Jim and Sammy and said, "I'm part of the construction crew that's building the new apartment wing over there." His "over there' was referring to the west side of the property where the apartment company was adding a new twenty unit wing, or building, —since it is not attached to another building.

"A few days ago, during lunch, Bruce, one of the other workers made a comment about how he thought this complex must have a lot of gay guys in it, and the rest of us sitting there kind of agreed. We had noticed quite a number of guys together and kind of acting like they belonged together. So anyway, we started keeping a watch, and we kept noticing more and more. Well, that kind of lead into some conversations about why guys do each other and wondering just what was so good about it. I guess none of us have ever done something with a guy, and the conversations got kind of wild and I guess started making some of us think about it. One thing led to another, and the whole group of us, about eight of us, decided that we wanted to see just what was so good about guy on guy sex."

Jim and Sam each looked at each other and grinned.

Sam looked at Chuck, and this time with a rather new eye of intent, —so to say. He uttered an interesting "Oh?" and then said nothing more. Suddenly Sam was a little more interested in just what Chuck looked like and was built like. Mental notes: Age, probably about 29 or 30. Definitely a construction worker body, big arms, big chest, little waist, and from what he could tell from his position, —nice ass. Probably about six foot even and maybe 185 to 200 pounds. His interest was now a little higher than just a few moments ago.

"And so what then happened?" Jim asked with more than just a little bit of anxious interest!

"Well, anyway, for a few days we all kept talking about it whenever we were together, and we kept wondering just what we were gonna do, or were we gonna do anything to answer our questions. It kind of got to be a major topic of conversation, and I do think that could be because I've always wondered about a couple of 'em anyway. I've kinda wondered if maybe they were keeping this talk going in the hopes that something would happen. I think a couple of 'em are really hoping somebody will set something up so they can do something, and not feel like they were the ones asking for it!"

Suddenly Sam interrupted and asked, "Chuck, you keep "saying" we, just who is the "we". Who are these guys? Tell me about 'em."

"Well there's me. And I already mentioned Bruce, he's the lead guy on the team, work-wise that is. He's kinda like the boss. He's older than the rest of us, I think he's probably about 45 or so."

"Bobby, he's the black guy! He's a hoot! He's really fun to work with. I think he's probably 23 or 24. Gotta tell you guys, you know Jack, the maintenance guy that works here, —yeah, the one that told me to come talk to you two guys, well Bobby is built almost like that Jack guy. And I will tell you that if I thought for a moment that I could get in the pants of that Jack guy, that maintenance man, —that is the one that I'd go for in a second! Damn he is hot looking, he has got the body of death on him, and I know some of the other guys think so too. I know he's straight, —he's married, —but damn man, I'd love to see him in a shower all naked and bare sometime! He's got one hell of a body on him, but hey, I guess you two have noticed that before since you're gays, and I do know gays check out other guys! Bobby is shorter than him, but just about as hot! "

"Uhh, Chuck, let me interrupt you here for a second." Jim entered. "Jack, —how do you know Jack, and how did it happen that he told you to come talk to us? Explain that to me, will ya?"

"Oh yeah, —yeah. Well, you see, one day when the whole group of us were having our lunch time conversation about guys doing guys and wondering all about that, Josh, he's another one of us, saw Jack walking from one building to another, and for some stupid reason, gotta admit I wouldn't have had the nerve to do it, Josh went over to Jack and ask him if there were a lot of gay guys living here, and Jack said yeah, he thought so. Well, Josh then told Jack that he wanted to meet some of 'em, and that's when Jack just told him to "go talk to the guys in apartment 117." I guess Jack must have assumed that since you two lived together that you were both gay. You guys are gay, —right? I mean, God I hope so after what I've been saying!"

Sam looked at Chuck, which he had been doing quite intently anyway, and answered, "Yeah Chuck, yeah! Jack was right, we're gay.

I guess maybe it's a little more obvious to everybody than I realized." He then looked at Jim and let out a very large grin. Unspoken statement of: "secrets man, secrets!"

"So did Jack say anything else about us, or to just come talk to us?" Jim asked.

"No he didn't say anything else. Just to come talk to you guys if we wanted to meet some of the gays that live around here. Actually he told Josh to come talk to you, but Josh was afraid to. Not afraid to go ask the maintenance guy about if there were gays living here or not, but too scared to come talk to you, so I said I would. I saw that Jack guy today, and I wanted to be sure Josh had the right apartment number, so I got the guts up to tell him I was gonna make the visit he suggested to Josh, and I wanted to make sure I had the right apartment number. That's how he knew I wanted to stop by tonight. I didn't know he was gonna call you though. I guess maybe he just wanted to make sure you were gonna be home tonight. Anyway, — here I am."

"Yeah, apparently." Sam added. "So you were telling us about the group. You, boss man Bruce, the black guy, what, —you said his name is Bobby, right?"

"Yeah, he's Bobby, —funny guy, —love to be around him, and then there's Mike. Mike is nice, but real quiet. He's like the youngest one on the group. I think he's 20 or 21. Oh yeah, he's 21. I remember a few weeks ago about how glad he was that he could now legally go into a bar and buy a beer. Said he had just turned 21 about three weeks earlier! Mike's tall. He stands about six foot three or four. He's the one we yell for when we need something held up high."

"Oh yeah, Josh! He's the one that asked that Jack guy about the gays living here. He's mixed. Black daddy and a white mommy, so he's said. All I can say is, regardless of what race they are, they both gotta be pretty people! I don't usually tell other guys that I think a particular man is, —well good looking, but since I'm talking to you gay guys, I guess it's okay! Josh, —he needs to be in movies! He is one handsome guy! I think he's 28, but not too sure. Told me he used to be a weight lifter in high school, and it looks like it. I think that's part of why I think he needs to be in movies. Face like that, and a body to go with it, he would be good in love scenes! Hey, maybe even some good porn too. Yeah, he'd really be good in porn. Straight or gay, either one. I've only seen a couple of gay porns, but I could see him doing that! Well anyway, he'd look good doing that!"

"Let's see, did I tell you about Dean? Now him I'm not too sure of, if he wants to carry through with this or not. He ain't said too much, just kinda sits there, but never says anything negative about what we say."

"Uhhhh, Chuck." Jim rather interrupted. Let me ask you something here. Okay? You just mentioned, if he wants to carry through with this or not. Maybe I'm a little dense, but carry through with what? I'm kinda confused here."

"Oh, each of us getting together with a man and finding out what gay sex is all about. I'm sorry, I guess I thought you already knew that. Yeah, we decided that we all want to have some sex with a guy, to see if we like it or not. We know the high school kids are taking a much more open attitude about gays and gays getting together, so we decided that maybe we needed to find out about it ourselves! I'm sorry, I guess I just assumed you knew that's what we were trying to get set up here."

Both Sammy and Jim reacted with a large smile on their faces and a very big, "Oh! Okay! Did not quite understand that part, I guess!"

Jim then asked. "Uh Chuck, just how many of you guys are married guys. Some of you married daddies?"

"Oh! Oh yeah! I'm single, not married. Raul, the Mexican guy, he's single. Mike, the guy I said is real quiet, he's single, Josh the guy that I think is so good looking, he's single, but the rest are all married, and some of 'em have kids.

Sam then asked, "So Chuck! You're telling me that the married guys, they wanna do the gay sex thing too?"

"Yeah, I guess! They all acted like they wanted to be part of this when we were all talking about it. Especially Bobby, the black guy. The guy I told you is really built, built kinda like that Jack guy! Yeah, for some reason he acts like he's really anxious for us to get this set up. He got married real young I guess, and I gotta admit, from the way he talks, I've wondered ever since he and I have been working together, wondering if he's sorry he's married to a woman. He really watches the guys, like how they move and how they bend over and all that stuff. I swear, every time that Jack comes around, Bobby almost quits working. I've seen him actually follow that Jack guy around some, as much as he can get away with anyway!"

"Chuck, you mentioned a Mexican guy. Raul, I think you said, right?" Sam asked. "What about him? Tell me about him."

"Of yeah, Raul! He's nice. He's more on the chunky side, I guess you could say. He's probably about 27 or 28 and I think maybe he eats too much cheesy stuff. He keeps bitching about how he needs to loose weight, but then eats like he's eating for two!"

"So like about how much does he weigh?" Jim asked with somewhat of a small frown on his face.

"Oh, I'd guess maybe about 230 or maybe a little more."

"Well how tall is he?"

"I'd say he's probably about five ten or eleven. I guess, but I'm not too sure. He just looks a little too heavy though."

"Okay, we've talked some about you, that Bruce guy, the quiet Mike, the good looking Josh and then Raul, is there anybody else in your group that wants to be part of this?"

"Oh yeah, Dean and Wayne. Dean, he's a former high school football player. He's, I think, 30, and yeah he's got a good body on him, but I gotta wonder if it's as good as he thinks it is. He was one of the original guys to be talking about the gay guys around here, cause I just know Dean is real sure all of 'em, the gay guys, will wanna take him and do him. I'm sorry, but I just think Dean is a little more stuck on himself than he needs to be. Oh yeah, then there's Wayne. He's one of the married guys, like Dean, and he's admitted a number of times that he's always wondered what sex with a guy would be like, but he's never done it. Of course he made all of us swear to secrecy if we do this. He told us there is no way in hell he can let his wife know what he did. And of course, we had to make a real pledge to him and all the rest of the guys, that if we do get something lined up to where we do this, everything has got to be totally secret. Hey, we even mentioned that if some of us go through with it, and maybe some don't, that is our business only, and not to be talked about unless the one that did it wants to. This is really doing something kind of way out of the ordinary and we gotta respect each other and keep our mouths shut. Well—I mean, not talk about it!"

"How old is that Wayne guy, did you say? Or did I forget?" Sam asked.

"Oh Wayne, I think he is probably about 35 or so. He's taken care of himself, and he looks good. I guess I mention that cause I've always heard that gay guys like to find and have sex with guys that are pretty well built and look good. Right?"

Shaking his head up and down some, Jim rather agreed, "Well yeah, I guess. Not all the time. But, sometimes."

"So what do you guys think?" Chuck asked. "Do you guys think that maybe you can help us get together with some guys? You think some guys might be interested in playing around with us some?"

"Well, I don't know! What do you think Sam?" Jim asked, but somewhat not with too serious of a tone.

Looking at Chuck, Sam then asked, "Well Chuck, just when did you guys want to get something going? What was your ideas? Can you say?"

Looking back to Sam and also over toward Jim, Chuck said, "Well, I don't know. I guess maybe I was going to kinda hope that you guys could give me some direction on that, well that is if you think something is possible! Do you think something is possible? Do you think something could be worked out?"

Grinning kind of widely, Jim shook his head up and down and looking at Sam, he then asked, "Well Sam, what do you think? Think maybe we could help these guys out, finding out if guy-to-guy sex, is as good as they think it might be?"

"I think so man, I do. And you know what?"

"What Jim?"

"I think we could get everything started right now, —don't you?"

"Hell yeah man! Hell yeah!"

Then looking over at Chuck, Jim asked, "So what do you say guy? You ready to get this started? You ready?"

Looking very confused, Chuck looked back at both Jim and Sam and asked, "Now!? You mean now? Is that what you're saying? You mean doing something right now? Is that what you mean?"

"Hell yeah man, hell yeah!" Jim replied.

"You ready? You want to try gay man-to-man sex, right? We're ready! Come on, let's go to the bedroom and see just how things go. Okay? Why put it off? You are one of the guys that wants it, aren't you?"

Looking rather flustered and kinda confused, Chuck did answer, "Yeah, yeah, but I didn't expect anything this fast! You mean now?'

Jim stood up, Sam stood up, and slowly Chuck stood up and then stated, "Shit men, I didn't expect it to get started tonight! You guys really serious, you mean now?"

Sam looked at Chuck, reached over, grabbed ahold of Chuck's crotch and said, "Yeah man, yeah! Yeah, we're serious, and right now I'm getting kinda anxious to see just what is hidden inside of here. The more I feel it, the bigger it's getting. Come on man, let's go to the bedroom, —I wanna taste me some construction man tonight, I do!"

All three men headed for the bedroom. Jim and Sam stripped down, and Sam then helped Chuck finish getting his pants and shoes and socks off. He worked a little slower than the other two. As he shed the rest of his clothes, he acted very embarrassed standing there and showing a very nice nine inch hard on.

Looking over at Sam, Jim stated, "Well man, it sure looks to me like maybe we started with probably the one that is most anxious to see just what man to man sex is all about, doesn't it? Look at that stick he's supporting."

Sam moved over to the edge of the bed, took ahold of Chuck's waist, pulled him up close and sank his mouth down and onto Chuck's cock.

"Oh shit, oh shit!" Chuck let out with, as he felt the back of Sam's throat hitting the tip of his rod!

"Oh shit man, oh wow! Oh man, that feels good, really good!"

As Sam was in the process of taking care of Chuck's cock, Jim reached up and slightly took a tit into each hand. Softly he squeezed and watched Chuck look up toward the ceiling and let out a very deep moan of pleasure.

"Oh so you like that right man?" Jim asked rather aimlessly! "Getting your tits played with while your cock is getting sucked feels good don't it? Now you know what some of that man to man sex feels like that you guys have been talking about don't you? Feels good don't it?"

Chuck brought his head back down, looked at Jim and shook an emphatic, "Yes." Then he managed a, "Oh yes man, oh yes! Oh guys, this is unbelievable! Oh shit man, oh shit!"

Sam continued to suck on Chuck's nice steel rod, and at the same time, Jim moved around to the back of Chuck, reached around front again and again took a tit in each hand, and at the same time slid down Chuck's back with his tongue and his chin until he was down, right at Chuck's butt. He pushed his face forward, spreading Chuck's ass cheeks and slid his tongue up and in the crack.

All of a sudden, Chuck let out with a big and powerful, "Oh my God man! Oh my God! I gotta shoot man, —I gotta shoot! I'm gonna cum guys, I'm gonna cum! Guys, —guys, —I gotta shoot guys, I gotta shoot!"

Sam knew what he was yelling, and he pulled him in, up close and tight, and Jim pulled back from having his face buried in Chuck's ass and said, "Shoot man, shoot! Let it fly! Let it fly! Sam wants it man, Sam wants it!"

Without any further comments or demands, Chuck let out one great big "Oh my God man!!! Oh shit man, —here it comes, —I'm cummmmmmin, —I'm cummmmmmmmmin! Oh shit man, that felt so fucking good! Oh man, I can't believe I shot like that! Oh shit man alive, —I'm fucking exhausted! God man, —I'm exhausted! Oh shit man, I feel like a canyon just shot off in me! Oh man, I shot like hell, I know I did! I know I did!"

Jim let loose of Chuck's tits, stood up and put his hands on Chuck's shoulders, and Sam slowly and lickingly slid off of Chuck's still hard and firm cock. Looking up at Chuck, Sam said, "Hey man. Construction cum tastes pretty damn good! No sawdust taste to it at all! You okay Chuck, you okay?"

Standing there, breathing deep, trying to get some breath back, Chuck rested his hands on Sam's shoulders and said, "Oh crap men, I had no idea! No fucking idea at all! I can not believe that, I can't. Hell guys, we've only been in here for what, less than three minutes and you guys have done that to me, that fast! Shit man, when I have straight sex it takes me a hell of a lot longer to hit a cum spot than that! Man, I've never shot off that fucking fast before, never! And shit man, I've never, never shot off that fucking strong before, never! I've never felt like my whole body was shooting off, and not just my dick! Oh shit man, —that was fucking great man, great! I can not believe it, I can't!! Wow, I guess all of our talking about gay sex sure ain't no fucking lie is it? Damn, shit, —what in the hell can I say? Hey guys, is it okay if I tell the other guys about this tomorrow? Can I tell 'em what it's like? Can I?"

After just a few minutes of re-grouping and rather re-gathering themselves, and both Jim and Sam telling Chuck that is gonna be okay for him to tell the other guys what happened, all three of the men jumped into the shower and freshened up.

Once they all dressed, Sam and Jim told Chuck to come back the next day, and they'd give him some input as to how they planned on getting each of the other guys with a gay guy, —so they could find out for themselves, what Chuck had just found out!

As they finished, Chuck looked at the two men that he had just had some great unexplainable sex with and said, "Oh shit! What in the hell am I gonna tell Sandra tonight after we get home from the club? I know she's gonna expect sex again, just like always before I take her home. Even if we do have sex, I'm gonna be wishing I was back here, doing it with you two, instead of in bed with her! Guys, I gotta be honest, after that, sex with her is gonna be meaningless, totally meaningless! There is no way in hell that I can feel like this, after sex with her, —no way in hell!"

CHAPTER TWELVE:

Jack, Which One do You want?

"Hey Jack, thanks man, thanks. I didn't know if you were gonna be able to stop in or not, but thanks!"

"So that Chuck guy did stop by last night, I assume, right?"

Jim looked at Jack with one hell of a big grin and said, "Yes, oh yes! Jack did you know why he wanted to stop in here and talk to us? Did you know?"

"Well, all I knew is that he and another guy, that Josh guy I think his name is, they were wanting to meet some gay guys, so I told 'em to come talk to you guys. That's all I knew. Why? Everything okay, everything okay?"

"Oh yes Jack! Everything is okay, more than okay!" Sam emphatically stated! "Yeah you are right, Chuck and Josh want to meet some gays, but, —hang in there man, —wait for this, — they are only two of a total of eight, —yes, —eight! That whole group wants man to man sex. That is what that Chuck came over here to talk to us about. He was asking for some help in getting that set up! None of them, supposedly, has ever had any gay sex, and the whole group has decided that they want to see what it is like! But Chuck now knows! Doesn't he Jim, —doesn't he?"

"Oh yes man, —yes he does! And we know how he is built and how he is hung, don't we Sam?"

Sam and Jim told Jack about the entire conversation and the rather short but good and exploding session with Chuck! The also told him that the construction crew has no idea at all that he does play with guys, or as Chuck has already implied, he would have been after Jack before this. All three had a good laugh about how none of the construction crew knew about how accessible Jack was to some guy that wants sex, and how Jim and Sam acted the dumb roll concerning that situation. They told Jack they wanted to be sure it was okay with him, before they let that whole group know he is as hot in bed as just walking around the apartment complex.

They talked about what Chuck had said about each of the guys, and also decided that to do this right, what they were gonna do is have Chuck get a time from each of the guys as to when they could come by for some play. Then after they had the list of times, decide just who was gonna be the playmate.

They told Jack that he was gonna get first dibs on which of the guys he wanted, if he knew which guy was which. So Jim asked him, "Jack, which one do you want? Do you know yet?"

"Oh yeah man, oh yeah! I get that little short black guy! The guy with all the muscles on him. Whatever his name is, I get him!"

Jack knew the Bobby guy from seeing him around the construction site, and made sure that Jim and Sam knew he had to be the playmate for that guy. Jack told them that since day one, with the crew on site, he had been huffing and puffing over that Bobby, and probably just about as much as Chuck said Bobby had been huffing and puffing over Jack.

Jack told Jim and Sam, that whatever time that Bobby said he would be available, he would be available too. If it meant even saying that he had to do something at the complex late some night, he would. He was very straight forward in telling the guys, that he was gonna show that muscle boy just what it felt like having another big black man, laying on his back and using his chute as a safety deposit box for his big long slonger! He told Jim and Sam that if for any reason they could not use their apartment for that get together, he was willing to take Bobby to some motel, —somewhere, —anywhere, where he was going to get that guy, and was going to really enjoy him!

"I have watched that little black man everyday he's been here, and there was no way in hell that I ever thought I would get a chance at him! He is gonna be my second black man! Yeah, me, —a black man, and he is gonna be only my second one to play around with, and get to slam dunk my dick up into! Damn man, this is gonna be good! Now wait guys! Sex with you two is really good, really good, —but admit it, —if you had a chance with that little black hunk of beef, you'd go for it too! Right?"

Grinning back at Jack, Jim reminded him, "Hey you're gonna get him first, but unless you scare the hell out of him and he doesn't want sex with a guy ever again, then we are gonna be next! Before he leaves that construction job, we're gonna have it too, —bet on it! He is too fucking hot to pass up on! Chuck has already told us that he wonders if Bobby is sorry he got married to a woman, and hey,—we just might help him decide if he did do the wrong thing or not! That is if you don't scare the hell out of him with that fucking telephone pole you call a dick!"

"Hey guys, we've all heard about how everything went with all of the other guys. Some good, like our, three times with Chuck, and then some not so good as with Bruce and Terry, and Bruce thinking he was still the boss, even though not on the job, and then of course Dean, all stuck on himself to where Jerry was just damn glad he was done, once he shot off in Dean's ass!" Jim kinda of reported as they were attempting to rather state the good and the bad of how the "get togethers" had gone, from what Chuck had come back and reported to them, earlier in the day.

"Hey, I heard that Dougie and Raul really did hit it off quite good!" Sam added. "Chuck said that Raul was really kinda "taken" by Dougie, so I'm glad I gave him a call to see if he wanted to be part of this. I'll have to call him and get a report from his side. Fact is, I need to call all of the guys that we don't see very often and find out how their sessions went."

"You guys know," Jim entered as Sam finished, "—from what Chuck said, everything with the unmarried guys went really well, but not so much for the ones where the men were with the married guys. Jack, you had a married guy, it's report time from you. How'd it go?"

"Yeah Jack," Sam stated as he looked over at Jack. "It's report time! You and "Little Bobby," as you call him, finally did your thing, —since he's now back to town from what, —a wrestling tournament that he was involved in, right?"

"Yeah, he's part of some wrestling group, and he did a three day trip to Philly for that. He came in second, so I think he must have done pretty damn well! Anyway, yeah, we finally got together last night. Thanks for letting us use your place. I appreciate it. I really do!"

"Hey why not? Sam and I had that graduation party for his niece to go to anyway, so hell, I'm glad the timing worked out. But tell us, —tell us, what about Bobby? Hot as you thought?"

"Oh hell yes man, hell yes! He told me that he had been with a guy once, many years ago, and the chance to do this was something that he'd wanted for a hell of a long time. He told me that when you guys told him I was gonna be his playmate, he almost kissed both of you guys! He had no idea that I could be approached, —no idea at all! And of course, neither did I, —that I could have just told him that I wanted to do him."

"So Jack, did you screw him? Did you? Would he let you?"

"Oh yes man, hell yes! And guess what! That fucker is hung bigger then me!"

"What, what!" Jim almost screamed. You are kidding right? You are kidding, right?"

"No honestly man, I am not! He only stands right at five foot nine, and he is swinging more than me. I have never sucked on a dick that large before, honestly, I never have!"

"Jesus Jack, —did he fuck you? Did you get him to fuck you?"

"Oh yes! Oh yes! Jim, I think he was in me for probably a full forty five minutes or more. I have never been fucked with a dick that big, and now I know why guys are always begging me to slam it up in their asses! Damn man! I will tell you that is the best feeling that I have ever had! Fucking good, fucking good! To be real honest guys, I kinda think that through this whole little process of those eight guys all wanting to try some gay guy sex, I just kinda think that maybe that Bobby and I both have found someone that we can each rely on whenever we need some good man to man friendship! We really did a hell of a lot more than just have sex last night! We bonded! I think we bonded like it takes most people years and years to bond like! I know it's sudden, but already we are a hell of a lot more than just fuck buddies! Last night we both said that we felt like we have known each other for our entire lives. We feel like we know stuff about each other that we've never even discussed."

"We're gonna keep doing our thing, —you guys and me, —Bobby knows that, but he and I, —I kinda think, we have each found somebody new, for a new kind of a friendship! I think he and I have both been looking and hoping for a new person in our lives. A person to fill some pretty big voids that we both feel, and I think that has now happened! I really do! A big thing, —a whole new relationship, —came in a very small way! Just a couple of hours together, and I think it's changed a lot for two guys that maybe are living the wrong way! We know, —we've both got our own personal lives to handle, but I think we can do it! I know we can! We'll do it! We mean too much to each other already! Thanks guys! Thanks for letting us use your apartment! Good ole apartment 117, I will remember you and this place forever! Thanks guys! Thanks!"

ABOUT THE AUTHOR

Wade Wright

Wade Wright is a semi-retired father of two daughters and four grandchildren. Following his marriage of twenty years, he did enjoy six and one half years with his first lover, which ended prematurely with a fatal case of pneumonia. A year later he gained the acceptance of his second lover, a very well built black man, —*now you will notice the similarities between his life and the lustings in many of his writings,* —and unfortunately, lost that love un-expectantly due to a fatal asthma attach. Since that loss, he has been living vicariously through the lives that he creates in his writings, and of course in his mind! His first lover was twelve years younger than he, and the second was twenty years younger, so he has no problem lusting after the young, the active, the well built, and usually the black, gay man!